Seven-Year Seduction

HEIDI BETTS

MILLS & BOON®

First published in Great Britain 2007
Large Print edition 2007.
Mills & Boon Limited, Eton House,
18-24 Paradise Road, Richmond, Surrey, TW9 1SR

© Heidi Betts 2006

ISBN-13: 978 0 263 19848 5
ISBN-10:   0 263 19848 0

Set in Times Roman 16¾ on 20¾ pt.
34-0307-45744

Printed and bound in Great Britain
by Antony Rowe Ltd, Chippenham, Wiltshire

HEIDI BETTS

An avid romance reader since junior high school, Heidi knew early on that she wanted to write these wonderful stories of love and adventure. It wasn't until her freshman year of college, however, when she spent the entire night reading a romance novel instead of studying for finals, that she decided to take the road less travelled and follow her dream. In addition to reading, writing and romance, she is the founder of her local Romance Writers of America chapter and has a tendency to take injured and homeless animals of every species into her central Pennsylvania home.

Heidi loves to hear from readers. You can write to her at P.O. Box 99, Kylertown, PA, 16847 (a SASE is appreciated but not necessary) or e-mail heidi@heidibetts.com. Be sure to visit www.heidibetts.com for news and information about upcoming books.

To my extremely talented
web designer, Shelley Kay, who does
such a wonderful job of keeping
my tiny corner of cyberspace neat,
beautiful and up-to-date. Thank you
for always coming up with solutions
to my problems and for never losing
patience with me, even after a
million-and-one silly little questions.

And to Su Kopil of Earthly Charms,
for being so helpful with my
promotional needs and desires,
and who also never seems to lose
patience after a million-and-one
silly little questions.

And always, for Daddy.

ACKNOWLEDGMENTS

With extra thanks to the PASIC Loop
for helping me with some of the
research for this book—especially
Lori Handeland, Sharon DeVita and
Shelley Galloway. You made my job
so much easier, thank you!

One

"**Y**es! Go, go, go!"

Fans went wild as the running back for the Crystal Springs Panthers raced across the field, making a touchdown and scoring extra points just as the buzzer sounded, winning the game for his team. Everyone on the home team's side of the bleachers jumped to their feet and began to cheer.

Beth Curtis joined them, yelling and bouncing up and down in celebration of her former high school's football team winning against their greatest rivals. Grinning from ear to ear, she turned and threw herself into the arms of the person on her immediate right—who just happened to be Connor Riordan.

Connor was five years her senior—the same age as her brother, Nicholas—but from the time she'd turned thirteen, she'd used any excuse to be closer to him, to be the focus of his attention and that coffee-brown gaze that made her weak in the knees.

She pressed her face to his cheek and rubbed against its sandpaper roughness. Even though it was practically freezing, and they were both wrapped up in heavy coats, hats, scarves and mittens, she could smell the musky scent of his evergreen cologne.

God, she loved that smell. Sometimes, when she and her girlfriends took a break from studying the law and all its many intricacies at the University of Cincinnati Law School, they'd take a trip to the mall. Beth almost always found

herself standing in the men's fragrance depart-
ment, sniffing at the colorful bottles until she
found one that smelled the most like Connor.

She suspected he wore Aspen, but couldn't be
positive without seeing the actual bottle he
likely kept on his bedroom dresser. But she was
working hard at finding out for sure.

Along with acing her next exam, one of her
objectives was to seduce Connor and make her
way not only into his bedroom but into his bed.
She'd had this aspiration since somewhere
around her senior year of high school, but now
she was an adult and there was no reason why
she and Connor couldn't become lovers. She
had been saving herself for him, after all.

He set her back on her feet, still grinning with
the thrill of victory as he brushed an errant
strand of hair away from her face.

As willing as the crowd had been to sit in the
stands for more than two hours to cheer on their
favorite team, they were just as eager to leave

now that they knew who'd won. People began collecting their seat warmers and empty cocoa cups and filing out of the stands.

"Hey, Curtis," Connor called over her head to her brother, who had his arm around his longtime girlfriend, Karen Morelli. "We going over to Yancy's for burgers?"

"Nah. Karen and I thought we'd head home. She wants to go shopping in the morning and we need to get an early start." Nick rolled his eyes, letting his friend know just how much he was looking forward to that.

"I could go for a burger," Beth put in quickly, seizing the opportunity to be alone with Connor.

It took him a minute, but finally he agreed. "Okay." He tossed a look at Nicholas. "I'll drop her off after we get a bite to eat."

"Sounds good." Karen and Nick shuffled single file to the end of their row, leaving Beth and Connor to follow.

When they reached the jam-packed parking lot,

Nick and Karen headed for his car while Beth stuck with Connor as he ambled toward his truck. The cold night air chilled her fingers, even inside their gloves, and caused her cheeks to tingle.

"*Brr.* It sure is cold tonight."

"Yeah." Connor unlocked the driver's side, then leaned across the seat to push open the passenger-side door. "Get in and I'll crank up the heat."

Beth eagerly climbed in and fastened her seat belt, holding her hands up to the vents as warm air began pouring out. They crawled like ants toward the exit of the school parking lot, vehicles each taking turns as everyone tried to squeeze out at the same time. Connor turned on the radio and tuned it to a Martina McBride song in an attempt to fill the silence in the pickup's cab and drown out some of the shouts and horn blasts from surrounding cars.

"Yancy's is going to be crowded," Beth pointed out, knowing that just about everyone went there after a game, whether it was to cheer another win for the Panthers' season, or to commiserate over a well-played loss.

Connor slanted her a glance as the car ahead of them eased forward. "I thought you were hungry."

She shrugged a shoulder, leaning back against the seat now that she was no longer chilled.

"Want to go someplace else?"

Taking a deep breath and swallowing down any remaining nerves bouncing around in her stomach, she said, "How about Makeout Point?"

He responded with a bark of laughter, followed by a dark, wide-eyed stare that clearly told her he thought she'd lost her marbles. "You can't be serious."

"Why not? I know why people usually go up there, but it really is a beautiful spot, and there aren't likely to be any teenagers up there tonight, getting themselves into trouble. They'll be too busy celebrating at Yancy's."

"What would your brother say if he found out I took his baby sister up to Makeout Point?"

Her teeth ground together at the mention of being "the baby sister." That was something she heard way too often for her peace of mind.

She wanted to tell Connor she didn't much care what her brother might say—she was an adult now and it was her life. But she knew how Connor felt about Nick and her parents, and that he would never do anything he thought they'd find unacceptable, especially where she was concerned.

"It's not like we're going up there for some illicit purpose," she told him instead. "I just thought it might be nice to visit the Point on a night we're likely to see more than rocking backseats."

To her surprise, he chuckled. "I suppose you're right. Do you want to pick up some burgers to take with us?"

"Sure."

They followed the cavalcade of taillights through town to Yancy's, but hit the drive-thru instead of going inside with most of the other post-game customers. Even so, they sat in line for quite a while, joining in with the arm waves and honking horns as friends and neighbors passed by in the black and gold colors of the Panthers team.

Once their order was ready, Connor passed the bags and drinks to her while he paid, then rolled up his window and pulled back onto the road, in the opposite direction of most of the town's population. The scents of French fries and grilled hamburgers permeated the cab, and Beth couldn't resist opening one of the bags and sneaking a potato.

Connor tipped his head in her direction, catching her in the act. "No fair," he grumbled. "I'm hungry, too, you know."

With a laugh, Beth reached into the bag a second time, then lifted a French fry to Connor's lips. He opened his mouth and bit down, nipping the tips of her fingers to catch the entire fry.

A jolt of awareness shot through her hand and

straight to her center, where desire and sharp arousal pooled. She wondered if he felt even a fraction the same as she did.

If she was lucky, by the end of the night, she would find out.

They bumped along the dirt road that climbed up to the Point and Connor angled his truck to look out over the pine-dappled ridge that gave this spot its name. The drinks and bags of food sat on the bench seat between them as they divvied up the order. They ate quietly for a while, watching the clouds slip across the moon and over the tree line.

When they'd finished, Connor stuffed their garbage back into the white paper bag and shoved it behind the seat, presumably to be retrieved and thrown away later.

Beth folded one leg beneath the other, vinyl squeaking beneath her jean-clad bottom as she shifted slightly more in his direction. His legs were stretched out in front of him, as much as the truck's console would allow, and he had an arm slung over the steering wheel.

"So how's school going for you?" he asked after several minutes of awkward silence had ticked by.

"Good," she replied. "Some of the classes are kind of hard, but I think I'm doing okay."

"If I know you, you're doing better than just okay. And wait until you're finished. You'll be a big-time lawyer, ready to sue the pants off of anybody who crosses you."

"I'm not going to sue anyone. I'm going to defend them."

"Nah," he put in idly. "You can't make money that way, unless you defend the rich and famous. And they're usually guilty as sin."

"I don't care about money. I want to help people."

He grinned at her then, and she got the distinct feeling he was seeing her as a child again, instead of as a full-grown woman or potential love interest.

"I'm not a kid, you know, Connor," she told him, pulling her shoulders back and thrusting out her breasts. They might not be as impressive as her roommate's 32Cs, but they weren't too shabby.

"I know. You grew up real nice, Beth Ann."

She might have taken his comment as another insult, another reminder that he thought of her as nothing more than his best friend's baby sister, except for his tone. The words came out in a near whisper, and the look in his eyes stroked her straight down to her soul.

It was as vulnerable as she'd ever seen him. As close to being open to seeing her as a woman he might be able to have a relationship with.

Before he could come to his senses or she lost her nerve, Beth leaned in and pressed her lips to his. For a moment, he held perfectly still, not kissing her in return, but not moving away, either.

When she pulled back, he blinked, the expression on his face a cross between shock and curiosity.

"Beth…"

"Don't say it," she murmured softly, staying where she was, pressed close to him on the wide truck seat. The heat from his body seeped past his unzipped winter coat and permeated every inch of her exposed skin.

"I know how you feel about me," she hurried on. "I know you think of me as Nick's little sister, nothing more than a tagalong. But I'm all grown up now, and I want us to be together. To at least explore what there might be between us."

She waited a beat, expecting him to respond. Surprised he hadn't interrupted her midspeech already.

"Haven't you ever thought about it, Connor? Haven't you wondered what it might be like between us?"

Her heart was pounding in her chest like the high school's half-time marching band, and the tension in the air threatened to send the burger she'd eaten into revolt.

But the fact that Connor hadn't immediately begun to argue with her, hadn't physically returned her to the other side of the bench seat and started to drive her home, gave her a modicum of hope. Maybe her infatuation wasn't entirely one-sided. Maybe there was a chance he was interested in her, too.

"Connor," she breathed, struggling to draw oxygen into her lungs even as she moved in to once again align her lips with his. "Please."

A second ticked by, then another while he stared at her, the intensity of his gaze flashing over her hair, her cheeks, her lips, her eyes. And then he was kissing her. Willingly, passionately, without reservation.

His hands snaked under her jacket, molding to her waist and the undersides of her breasts even as she raised herself up on her knees. She hovered above him, trying to get closer, wanting to slide inside and become one with him.

She'd waited so long for this moment,

imagined dozens of times being with him this way. It was almost too much to believe, and a part of her thought she might be dreaming.

But then he pinched her nipple through her sweater, through the lace of her bra, and she knew it was blessed reality. Every fantasy she'd ever had about her brother's best friend was going to come true.

He tasted of cola and Yancy's special sauce from the burgers they'd eaten earlier, and smelled like the outdoors. He always smelled like the outdoors, and Beth thought it must be a combination of his own personal, masculine scent and his cologne preference.

She curled her fingers into the soft flannel of his plaid work shirt, skimming his coat off over his shoulders while he fought with the zipper on her own. Once he had it undone, he wasted no time getting her out of the fleece-lined jacket, tossing it to the floor of the cab.

His hands immediately returned to her hips,

where they rested for a moment before slipping under the hem of her sweater and gliding upward. The touch of his callused fingertips on the smooth expanse of her torso set off forest fires just beneath the surface of her skin.

It was cold outside, and should have been cold inside the truck by now, without the engine running. Instead, she felt hothouse warm, their mingled breaths fogging up the windows.

They were acting like a couple of randy teen-agers, and she didn't even care. Given half a chance, she'd have driven up to Makeout Point with Connor while she'd been in high school, too.

With a moan, his lips parted, leaving her mouth to trail over her chin, down the line of her throat. She arched her neck, granting him better access.

While his tongue flicked and teased, she worked the tail of his soft cotton T-shirt out from the waistband of his jeans. His abdomen tightened as she stroked it, exploring the rock-hard muscles and dancing her fingers over the light dusting of hair that ran from navel to chest and back down. She followed the trail to the edge of his jeans, deftly undoing the metal button at the top.

At the same time, his hands cupped her breasts, pushing the fabric of her bra up to delve beneath. Her beaded nipples pressed into his palms and when he rubbed, tiny shock waves of desire shot straight to her center.

His mouth moved back up, his lips brushing hers as he spoke. "We shouldn't be doing this. It's wrong."

"It's not wrong," she told him, catching his ears and kissing him deeply. "It's right. So very, very right."

He groaned, seeming to give in, regardless of any other arguments that might be crashing through his mind. He wrapped his arms around her and lowered her to the truck seat, following her down.

Her knee bumped the steering wheel as they

tried to find a comfortable position. His foot cracked into the door, his elbow hit the dash, she bumped her head on the opposite door handle. If they hadn't been so turned on, they might have given up altogether.

As it was, they laughed at their awkward positions, shifting until they each found a modicum of comfort. Then they were kissing again, lips meshing, tongues flicking, breaths mingling.

Connor curled his fingers on either side of her jeans closure and pulled the snap free. The *snick snick snick* of the zipper as he released it echoed through the cab. He shoved the pants down her legs, leaving them bunched somewhere around her calves rather than fight to get them off over her shoes. Her panties were next, followed by his trousers and underwear.

As much as Beth wanted this, had been wanting it for so long, the cool air on her lower extremities sent a thread of hesitation through her.

This was Connor. Her brother's best friend.

The man she'd been dreaming of being with ever since she'd hit puberty.

She wasn't sorry she'd gotten herself into this situation…if anything, she was relieved she'd *finally* managed to snag Connor's undivided and romantic attention. But she did know that sleeping with him would change things. Forever.

The way they looked at each other, the way they acted around each other. The way he acted around her family.

Of course, she hoped things would change for the better. That she and Connor would become an item after tonight, date for a while, get engaged, then marry and start a family.

A picture of them ten years down the road shimmered in her mind's eye and she smiled, even as Connor's fingers skimmed her inner thigh, making rational thought nearly impossible.

Whatever happened, they could handle it, and everything would be fine. He was already as close to Nicholas as a brother, as close to her parents as another son. Her entire family would be more than accepting of their relationship, and she knew that once Connor recovered from the shock of having slept with his best friend's little sister—if indeed he suffered any shock at all—he would realize they belonged together.

She'd finish law school, of course, then move back home to be close to him, and one day they'd be man and wife. One day they'd be living happily ever after.

Beth smiled for a brief moment, then whimpered when he grazed the curls between her legs with the back of his hand. He nudged her knees open as far as they would go with her jeans still wrapped around her ankles, then settled himself the best he could in the cradle of her thighs.

His palms stroked up and down her bare torso, her sweater pushed up around her breasts. She felt the tip of his hardened length probing intimately while his mouth continued to devour her own.

He was gentle but demanding, considerate but firm. One hand skated along her waist and hip, then cupped around her bare derriere and lifted her.

He slid inside more easily than she'd expected, given her state of virginity. But he was still big, and filled her until she had to tip her hips to find a more comfortable position.

Her legs were pressed against the steering wheel and back of the truck seat, and she could hear the rubber soles of Connor's work boots as they came in contact with the driver's-side door. His chest rose and fell with the heavy force of his breaths, in synch with her own.

When he thrust even deeper, she gasped, a slight burning assaulting her tender, innocent passage. He stopped moving and lifted his head, giving her time to adjust to his invasion.

"You okay?" he asked, looking down at her with eyes the color of melted chocolate, tiny beads of perspiration dotting his brow.

Her teeth sawed delicately on her bottom lip, more out of habit than any real pain. "I'm fine."

He didn't look as if he believed her, so she reached up to brush a loose lock of hair out of his eyes, a comforting smile lifting her lips.

"I'm fine, really." And then she wrapped her arms around his back and pulled him down. "But I don't think we're finished yet."

Seconds passed while strain continued to etch his face. Then suddenly, the lines tipping down his mouth lifted as he grinned back at her. "No, ma'am. We're just getting started."

His kiss was soft and tender as he took her lips and began moving his hips in a slow, steady rhythm. Friction built, like a length of silk being dragged over sandstone. The faster he moved, the tighter the coil of sweet tension grew, winding low in her belly until she wanted to scream.

And then she did, as the dam seemed to break and a keen, clawing pleasure unlike any she'd ever experienced before washed over her. She continued to shudder with tiny aftershocks while Connor rocked into her once, twice, three times more before going rigid with his own overwhelming completion.

They lay there for long minutes, struggling to regain their equilibrium. Connor's rough jaw tickled her cheek, his uneven breathing whispering in her ear.

Her arms and legs were still wound around him like strands of ivy, and the corners of her mouth lifted slightly at how right it felt to be with him this way. Even in the cramped confines of his truck cab, half dressed, half undressed, the evening was perfect. And there would be plenty of times in the future when they could strip off each other's clothes, take it slow, explore every inch of flesh before climbing under satin sheets and making long, languorous love all night long.

This was just the beginning.

Connor lifted his head, meeting her gaze briefly before pushing himself up and helping her to get untangled from his lithe form. He pulled her sweater down and waited until he was sure she could get her panties and jeans up by herself before righting his own clothing.

Neither of them said anything until they were each back on their own sides of the truck seat.

"Are you all right?" he asked in a low tone. He was looking straight out through the windshield, his fingers wrapped tight around the steering wheel.

"Yes. Are you?"

He didn't answer, just continued to face forward.

With a sigh, he leaned forward and twisted the key in the ignition. The engine turned over, and heat and music began to fill the cab.

"I'd better get you home," he told her. "Before your family starts to worry."

She nodded, knowing they would if she was gone too much longer. Then again, Nick knew she was with Connor, and they trusted him implicitly.

But she didn't blame him for feeling a bit uncomfortable; it might take time for him to get used to the idea of them being an item.

Which was fine. She'd let him take her home tonight, and they could sit down in the morning to discuss the future.

She studied him from the corner of her eye as they drove down the rutted road and away from Makeout Point. His strong jaw, dark blond hair, slightly crooked nose. The strong line of his shoulders and wide, muscled biceps.

This was the man she loved, had *been* in love with since her thirteenth birthday. And now he would be the man she married and spent the rest of her life with.

She couldn't wait.

Two

Seven years later...

Beth Curtis sat at the family table on the dais, sipping from her glass of champagne, watching as the bride, groom and dozens of guests filled the dance floor.

She hated weddings.

She was happy for Nick and Karen, really she was. They had been dating since high school, and she—and everyone else in town—knew they'd marry eventually. Of course, her brother had put off proposing right up until the stick turned blue. Regardless of their reasons for finally tying the knot, though, Beth had no doubt they would make it work. They belonged together.

But she still hated weddings. Especially this one.

Bad enough she'd been roped into being the maid of honor, with all the duties that position entailed. Bad enough she'd had to fly over two thousand miles each way to come back to Crystal Springs for the bridal shower, wedding and reception planning, and now the actual event. Bad enough that Karen's favorite colors were green and pink, and that Beth was therefore decked out in a formfitting satin sheath made up of lime and watermelon shades of each.

Oh, no, all that was bad enough. The worst, the very worst, was that she had to smile and laugh and pretend that seeing Connor Riordan again wasn't a dagger through her heart.

She'd done a pretty good job of avoiding him

since he'd taken her virginity all those years ago. Moving to Los Angeles had helped, as had not coming home to visit her parents and brother nearly as often as she might have liked.

And then Nick had decided he just *had* to do the right thing by marrying Karen because he'd gotten her pregnant, and Connor just *had* to be his best man. Which meant Beth and Connor had to see each other more than she'd have preferred. He even walked her down the aisle during the ceremony.

She took another swig of bubbling wine. It was warm and starting to lose its fizz, but she didn't care. The alcohol content would remain the same, and right now she wanted nothing more than to go numb.

Standing in the church's vestibule with Connor, his arm linked with hers while the soft notes of the wedding march played had been like a red-hot brand on her soul. He couldn't have known she was in actual physical pain, of course, and he had no idea that being around him was so hard for her…or why. But that didn't lessen the ache in the pit of her stomach or the harsh memories that ran through her head at the very mention of his name.

And now she was lucky enough to have a bird's-eye view of him dancing cheek to cheek with his live-in girlfriend. Laura, Lori, Lisa… something like that. She was blond and perky and had boobs that bounced when she walked. Beth would bet next month's salary that she'd been a cheerleader in high school. And that the bounce was saline- or silicone-induced.

Not that there was anything wrong with that. Beth was a California girl now; plastic surgery came with the territory. Heck, as an entertainment attorney who worked with some of Hollywood's most beautiful stars, the majority of her clients had been nipped or tucked in one way or another.

So why was she being so judgmental of Lisa-Lori-Laura?

Simple. She was with Connor and Beth wasn't.

Connor had apparently felt strongly enough about the L-woman to ask her to move in with him, when he hadn't felt enough for Beth to even pick up the phone and call her after their one night together in the cab of his truck.

Jealous? Yes, she supposed she was. But more than that, she was hurt and angry. No amount of time or number of miles between them would change that.

Seven years certainly hadn't.

Beth paused with the champagne flute halfway to her mouth. No, that wasn't quite true. She was over him. Absolutely, positively, one hundred percent over him.

The only feelings she still harbored toward Connor were ones of resentment. Just hearing his name raised her blood pressure. Not because she missed him or wished she could be his girlfriend, but because the thought of him made her want to strangle somebody when she didn't typically suffer from homicidal tendencies.

To some, those emotions might be welcome in relation to an ex-lover, but to her, they only served to remind her that he had had an impact on her at all. She hated that. Loathing was better than longing, but she'd prefer to be indifferent toward him.

"What are you doing hiding over here all by yourself? You should be dancing."

Her brother's voice came to her from over her left shoulder and she tipped her head back to look at him. Clear as a bell, steady as a surgeon… Damn, she was still sober.

"It's not my wedding day. I'm not required to make a fool of myself."

"Gee, thanks." He crossed his eyes and stuck his tongue out, mugging for her the way he'd done all her life. "Look, Karen's shoes are pinching her, but I'm still in the mood to dance, so I need a new partner."

Beth scanned the crowd and pointed toward an attractive brunette with the rim of her glass. "Ask her."

"Are you kidding me? If I danced with anyone but my sister, my new bride would divorce me before the honeymoon." He waggled his eyebrows. "And I'm really looking forward to that honeymoon."

It was Beth's turn to roll her eyes. "Please. It's nothing new to you two, and we both know it. So will everyone else in six or seven months."

"Shh. We're keeping that a secret as long as we can. Now get up and dance with me, or I'll think you aren't happy for your big brother's recent state of wedded bliss."

With a sigh, she set down her empty glass and pushed to her feet. "Well, we can't have that."

Nick grinned as he took her hand and led her onto the crowded dance floor. Rod Stewart's throaty version of "The Way You Look Tonight" was playing, but Beth refused to give the song's lyrics too much thought as Nick's arm wrapped around her and they began to sway.

"I really am happy for you, you know."

The corners of his mouth lifted in a grin. "I know. It took me a while to get here, but I'm awfully glad I did."

She chuckled. "If you didn't put a ring on Karen's finger soon, I think she was about ready to string you up. You have been dating since high school, after all."

"Yeah, but I wanted to make sure she loved me for me and not my millions."

Beth threw back her head and laughed. Nick was lucky he had two nickels to rub together. He and Connor owned a contracting company together and did a lot of the work themselves, but they weren't exactly raking in the dough. Early on in their partnership, there had been months when they barely broke even; more when they were clearly in the hole.

Things were better now, but neither of them

was rich by any stretch of the imagination. If Karen had truly been looking for a man with money to spare, she'd have run screaming from Nicholas years ago.

Beth, on the other hand, was doing pretty well for herself. Things had been tight when she'd first moved to L.A. The exorbitant cost of living on the West Coast, in addition to school loans that still had to be paid off, hadn't been easy to swing for a girl who didn't even have a job yet. She'd made ends meet at first by waitressing and temping at a few law firms.

Then she'd lucked out in finding a friend and fellow attorney who did have some cash to spare and was willing to form a partnership with her. Danny Vincent was a great guy. He came from money, so he'd been the one to foot all the start-up costs of Vincent and Curtis, but she'd done her best to pay him back by scouting out the talent, wooing new clients, and even stealing a few from other, more well-established firms.

The first few years had been backbreaking. She'd worked nonstop not only to prove herself, but to build the business so Danny never had a chance to think he'd made a mistake.

And now, they were pretty much set. They had high-profile celebrities and sports figures on their clientele list, with others waiting in line for their expertise, and the firm was operating well into the black on an annual basis.

She wore designer clothes, designer shoes, designer jewelry. A single trip to the salon cost her more than Karen probably spent on her hair in a year.

Which only served to make Beth feel even more removed from the small Ohio town where she'd been raised. She missed it sometimes…the friendly faces, the slow pace, her family. But that's what telephones and e-mail were for. She'd grown up and moved on. She was happy with her life.

The song ended and Nick started to let her go. One of the caterers had just placed a fresh bottle of champagne on the bridal table, and she wanted to get back to refill her glass.

"You're not running off already, are you?"

It wasn't her brother's voice that made her heart drop to her knees. Mentally, she closed her eyes and banged her head a couple of times against the nearest wall. But she'd been working with Hollywood bigwigs too long to let anyone see that she wasn't calm and one hundred percent in control of her emotions.

Licking her lips to buy an extra second, she forced herself to smile and turn in the direction of the loaded question.

"Hello, Connor."

He looked as handsome as ever. Better even, in his best-man tuxedo, when his usual uniform was well-worn blue jeans and soft flannel shirts. His hair was still barbershop short, no signs of gray in the brownish-blond strands. And his brown eyes twinkled as though he carried a secret no one else knew.

He did, of course. He knew what they'd done after the football game all those years ago, up at Makeout Point. She doubted he'd ever told anyone, though. She certainly hadn't.

"Hey, Beth. I meant to tell you earlier that you're looking good. L.A. must be treating you right."

She nodded. He didn't need to know about the small ulcer she'd developed from eighteen-hour workdays and a demanding clientele, or the antacids she kept in her purse for the occasional flare-up.

As far as the residents of Crystal Springs were concerned, she'd gone off to California and become a huge success. There was no sense in telling them things weren't always as silver lined as they seemed.

"Would you like to dance?" Connor asked when another slow song began to fill the reception hall.

With him? Definitely not. She opened her mouth to politely refuse, but he already had his hand curled around her upper arm, steering her into his embrace, and her brother seemed more than willing to pass her off.

"Great," Nick said. "You dance with Connor, and I'll get back to Karen."

"She's got you on a tight leash already, huh?" Connor joked, throwing her brother a guy-to-guy grin.

"You should try it sometime," Nick replied, tossing his friend an equally teasing smile before sauntering off.

It would have caused a scene if she'd pulled away and returned to the table at that point, even though that's exactly what she wanted to do. Instead, she continued smiling and allowed Connor to put an arm at her waist, entwine his fingers with hers.

Because she didn't have a choice, she slid her free hand up to rest on his shoulder. The heat of his body pulsed through the fine wool of his tuxedo jacket, setting her palm to tingling.

She muttered a colorful oath under her breath, annoyed that he could still have any sort of impact on her, even a purely physical one.

And that's all it was—the physiological response of her female body to the nearness of such an attractive, obviously male body. Their shared history added to her body's response, but it didn't mean anything. Nothing at all.

"How have you been, Beth? I hear you've done well for yourself out there in la-la land."

"I'm doing all right," she said shortly. "And you?"

"Couldn't be better. Nick probably told you the company's doing well, keeping us both busy. Things slow down in the winter, of course, which is the only reason I'm letting him take off on this two-week honeymoon of his."

He shot her a wide, sparkling grin. She didn't respond.

"So what do you think about your big brother finally tying the knot?"

"It's about time, I say. They've only been dating since they were in diapers."

"Yeah. Makes you wonder, though, how much longer he'd have put it off if Karen hadn't surprised him with her little announcement."

"I don't know," Beth told him, trying not to get too drawn in to the conversation…or the warmth of his hold on her…or the lulling sensation of the music and moving around the dance floor with him. "I think Nick just needed an excuse to jump in with both feet. He's been wanting to marry Karen since they were teenagers, but he had all those typical male fears and insecurities. They fell into a comfortable pattern after high school that kept him from having to put his heart on the line until now."

Connor was still smiling, that stupid boy-next-door smile that reminded her of exactly why she'd moved as far across the country as possible after her graduation from law school.

"That's awfully philosophical for a gal who

spends her days reading contracts and suing production companies," he remarked.

"Lawyers can be philosophical," she volleyed back. "We just prefer not to show that side of ourselves during billable hours."

Connor threw back his head and laughed at that, and Beth couldn't help but laugh with him. She'd forgotten how infectious his sense of humor was. How his low chuckle or full-belly laugh washed over her like a warm sea breeze.

When the moment passed, she found herself dancing even more closely to him. He'd somehow tightened his grip and brought her flush with his tall, muscular frame without her noticing. He took the lead as they swayed to an old Air Supply ballad, keeping a firm grasp on her so she couldn't slip away or even put space between them again.

Her breasts were pressed against his chest, and her damn, traitorous nipples began to pucker beneath the satin bodice of her lime green and hot-pink maid-of-honor gown. She only hoped he wouldn't notice through the thick material of his own formal attire.

"Remember that dance back in junior high," he said, "when your folks wouldn't let you go unless Nick and Karen and I went along?"

How could she forget? She'd convinced herself it was a real date, while to Connor, it was nothing more than a favor for his best friend's sister and her parents.

"We danced half the night just like this," he continued.

Not exactly like this, she thought as his pelvis brushed against hers, making her stomach muscles tighten and heat pool thick in her veins.

"I even think they played this same song," he said with a chuckle.

She didn't remember the music from that night so many years ago, only the feel of Connor holding her as they shuffled back and forth in the middle of the darkened gymnasium. Her complete adoration for the boy of her dreams had been embarrassingly clear on her face, she was sure.

Thank God she'd grown up and moved on. She was beyond the starry eyes and stupid, love-struck glances of adolescence. She was strong, independent, and over him.

As soon as the thought passed through her mind, she knew she had to exert a bit of that independence and get away from him. She didn't want to talk about junior high or high school. Or anything from their past, for that matter. Better to let those memories—not a one of them good for her—remain dead and buried.

Before the song even ended, she stopped cold and took a step back. He still held her hand, his other arm extended from her waist.

"What's wrong?" he wanted to know, but he didn't release her.

"Nothing. I just don't want to dance anymore."

"Then let's take a walk." His fingers clenched around hers for a moment before relaxing. "I'll get us something to drink and we can go outside for a breath of fresh air."

"Thank you, but no."

"Come on. Just for a few minutes."

She stopped trying to pull away from him then and simply stared him straight in the eye.

"Why?" she wanted to know, studying him closely. "Why won't you let me go back to the table and leave me alone?"

For a second, he didn't say anything. Then he gave a heartfelt sigh, letting one arm drop to his side, but keeping a grip on her other hand.

"Look, I know things have been weird between us the past few years. It doesn't take a genius to figure out that you do your best to avoid me every time you come home to visit your family, and I just thought that maybe we could talk. Clear the air a bit."

Clear the air. As soon as the words sank in, her hackles went up.

If only life were that simple. If only a breath

of fresh air and a few interesting stories about the good old days could wipe away all the pain, misery and anguish from that time in her life.

But they couldn't, and she had no desire to dredge up the past. Coming home for her brother's wedding had been difficult enough. Having a heart-to-heart with Connor was more than she could handle, more than she was *willing* to handle tonight.

She had been telling herself for years that she'd put him and everything that had passed between them behind her. Now seemed like the perfect time to prove it.

She yanked her hand from his, giving him no choice but to finally let go.

"There's nothing to talk about," she told him, leaving no room in her tone for argument. "Consider the air perfectly clear. Now, I'm going back to the bridal table to finish my champagne. And you should go back to your girlfriend."

She cast a glance over his broad shoulder,

toward the well-built blonde in a stylish burgundy sheath who'd been glaring at them for the past several minutes. "She doesn't look too happy that you've been dancing with another woman."

With that, Beth turned on her heel and walked away. She grabbed her empty glass and the fresh bottle of champagne from the table as she passed, deciding to catch that breath of fresh air, after all. Alone.

Three

Connor ran a hand over the top of his head, blowing out a frustrated breath. Well, that had gone just great.

He'd meant to smooth things over with Beth, try to repair their old but battered friendship, not piss her off all over again. Or even more, depending on how one looked at it.

And there had to be something seriously wrong with him to be staring at the tight curve of her bottom as she stormed away while she was so obviously annoyed with him *and* while Lori was watching.

He couldn't seem to help himself, though. Beth had been an adorable kid, an attractive teenager, and now, as an adult, she was drop-dead beautiful.

He cursed himself for thinking it, for noticing her feminine attributes at all. She was his best friend's sister and he was practically engaged to Lori, for God's sake. Or at least, they'd been living together for the past three years, and he knew that was what she expected.

But he was a man, and as much as he might wish it otherwise, he wasn't made of stone. Beth Curtis had eyes like the Hope Diamond—clear and bright and reflective. With one glance, she could either make him squirm or make him want, freeze him out or set fire to his belly and below.

She used to wear her chestnut hair in a ponytail or braid, but the older she'd gotten, the more she let it hang long and loose down her back. The wavy strands reminded him of the finest silk, and he wanted to run his fingers through them every time she was near.

And her body…man, her body had filled out like nothing he'd ever seen. Yeah, Lori was built. Tiny waist, long legs, big breasts. But her chest had been surgically enhanced, and as much as he'd enjoyed the benefits of that work, there was something about the idea of silicone or saline swishing around in there that turned him off. He would never tell Lori he felt that way, of course, but it was true.

Beth, on the other hand, was just as God had made her. And he'd done a damn fine job. She wasn't model thin or tall, but he liked that. He liked the way her breasts filled that awful pink-and-green gown without looking fake. He liked the curve of her waist, the flare of her hips, the sweet little behind the cut of her dress alluded to. He even liked the slim expanse of her ankle, visible above the strap of her pink, three-inch heels.

And that was why he was going straight to hell.

He pressed a finger and thumb to his eye sockets, thinking—not for the first time—that he was either crazy or the unluckiest bastard around to keep getting into these situations. Beth was practically family, but he couldn't seem to stop lusting after her.

Knowing he couldn't put it off any longer, he dragged his gaze away from Beth's retreating form and turned to face Lori.

Beth had been right, she didn't look happy. Which meant he'd managed to piss off two beautiful women in one night. That was a record, even for him.

She was sitting at the table where he'd left her, arms crossed over her ample chest, legs crossed, top foot tapping angrily in midair. A pulsing, upbeat dance number shook the floor beneath their feet, but the music failed to permeate Lori's sour mood.

Well, this should be fun.

He started toward her, but she leaped to her feet and met him halfway, fire brimming in her eyes.

"Hey," he greeted her, smiling and trying to pretend he didn't realize how upset she was.

"So that was her."

"Who?" Connor cocked his head slightly, hoping he would catch another glimpse of Beth before she disappeared too deeply into the crowd. No such luck.

When he turned back around, Lori's expression was even darker, brows drawn and lips pulled down.

"Her. She's the one."

"The one, who?" he asked, growing more confused by the minute.

"The one who's keeping you from making a commitment to me."

"Lori," he began, scoffing at her accusation.

"No," she cut him off. "I knew there was something going on. I knew there was someone or some incident you couldn't put behind you, but I had no idea it was *her.* Your best friend's sister."

She said the last as though it was the gravest of insults, and Connor once again felt his insides tighten with shame.

She was right. Beth was his best friend's sister—off limits, taboo. What he thought about her those times he couldn't control his raging hormones, and what they'd done all those years ago, was reprehensible.

And even though Lori had hit the nail on the head, he wanted to deny it. *Needed* to deny it.

"You don't know what you're talking about," he told her, sliding his hands into the pockets of his tux jacket. "Beth and I are friends. We grew up together. She isn't keeping me from doing anything."

"I *mean,*" she growled, leaning in to be heard over the music, but not by anyone else, "I saw the way you looked at each other. The way you held her while you danced. I'm not blind, Connor. There was more there than friendship. More than dancing with your best friend's sister."

"That's ridiculous."

"It's not." Her voice grew thick and tears glistened along her lower lashes. "It explains a lot, actually. Like why there's no ring on my finger," she said, holding up her bare left hand as proof. "And why I'm at your best friend's wedding instead of my own. We've been dating for six years, Connor. Living together for three. If that doesn't prove you have commitment issues, I don't know what will."

She turned her head in the direction Beth had earlier escaped. "Now I know why."

"Lori…"

"I don't think this is going to work, Connor. I

don't think I can live with you anymore, knowing I'm not the woman you really want to be with."

She walked to the table to gather her purse, then returned to stand in front of him. Without meeting his gaze, she murmured, "I don't think you should come home tonight. Maybe not ever."

It crossed his mind to tell her it was his house…she'd moved in with him, not the other way around. But this was hard enough on her. He'd never meant to hurt her, yet here she was, in obvious pain because of him.

His throat was too tight to speak, so he merely nodded.

He saw the hitch in her breathing before she straightened her shoulders and left the reception hall like a queen leaving a grand ballroom, head held high, regal to the core.

Damn, this night just kept getting better and better.

"Hey, buddy."

Nick came up behind him, slapping him on the

back and shoving a bottle of cold beer at him. Connor pulled a hand from his pocket and accepted the much-needed drink.

"Thanks, man." He took several long swallows before lowering the bottle.

"No problem. Trouble in paradise?" his best friend asked.

"Yeah. I think I just got kicked out of my own house."

"Ouch. You and Lori had a fight, then. What about?"

Nothing he could share with Nick.

"It's not important," he mumbled, hoping Nick wouldn't press for details.

He took another swig of beer, then dug into his pants pocket to feel for his wallet. "I hate to take off so early, but I'd better start looking for a hotel vacancy or I'm going to end up sleeping in my truck." Which he'd have to walk home to retrieve, since they'd driven to the wedding and reception in Lori's car.

"Listen," Nick told him. "Why don't you stick around a while longer, enjoy yourself, then you can crash at my place. Karen and I are heading straight for the airport after this and won't be back for two weeks. If you and Lori make up, great. But if you don't, you can stay there as long as you like."

"Are you sure?" Connor asked, touched by his friend's generosity. But then, the Curtises had always treated him better than he deserved.

Even as a rough-and-tumble foster kid from across the street, they'd invited him in and acted as if he was no different than Nick or any other boy their age.

Never mind that he was hell on wheels, with a chip on his shoulder the size of Texas, working on getting kicked out of his eighth or ninth foster home. They'd accepted him, trusted him, even grown to love him as much as he loved them.

His eyes grew damp just thinking about how accepting they'd been of him, despite the asinine things he'd done to test them. They'd changed his life, and if it took him until the day he died, he'd do everything he could to repay them.

"Mi casa es su casa," Nick quipped. "I'd feel better knowing someone was around, anyway."

"Thanks, man, I really appreciate it."

"No problem. Now, why don't you come on over to the table with us, and when we leave, we'll swing past your place so you can pick up your truck."

Connor cast a sideways glance at his friend as they negotiated the crowd and headed toward a smiling Karen, still decked out in her white wedding dress and veil.

"You're going to ride me about this after you get back from your honeymoon, aren't you?"

Nick snorted, not bothering to hide his amusement. "Oh, yeah. Getting dumped at my wedding, kicked out of your own house... It's too good to let go." He slung an arm around Connor's shoulders. "Don't worry, buddy, I'll still remember all the details when I get back."

Connor shook his head, rubbing at the headache that was beginning to form right between his eyes. "That's what I'm afraid of."

The scent of fresh-brewed coffee filled the air and tickled Beth's nose where it was buried in her pillowcase. She rolled to her back with a groan and slowly opened her eyes.

Well, the room wasn't spinning. That had to be a good sign.

She wasn't intoxicated—not anymore—but she was hungover. She could feel it, from the throbbing in her brain to the thick pile of cotton coating her tongue.

What had she been thinking? She'd left her brother's wedding reception with a full magnum of champagne and ended up drinking so much the bottle ached.

She never did that sort of thing, and it galled her to realize she'd let things get to her so much last night that she'd turned to alcohol to numb her emotions.

Thank God it was over, though. Nick and Karen would be on their honeymoon by now, or at least on their way to sunny Honolulu. And all of their guests would have gone home, Connor and his peroxide-blond girlfriend included. She never needed to see him again.

Life couldn't get much better.

She pushed herself out of bed and lurched to the connected bathroom, using the nightstand and dresser to keep from falling over. After brushing her teeth and splashing a little water on her face, she felt more human. She was even walking straighter as she made her way downstairs, following the mesmerizing fragrance of java and the promise of a jolt of caffeine.

Turning the corner into the kitchen, covering a yawn with the back of her hand, she opened her eyes to find a man standing at the counter with his back to her.

A yip of fear and surprise passed her lips before she could stop it, and the man whirled in her direction. If she hadn't been feeling so sluggish and out of sorts when she woke up, she might have figured out earlier that in order for her to smell fresh-brewed coffee, another body had to be in the house to make it.

And she'd been wrong: Life couldn't get much worse.

Connor watched her with wide eyes, just as stunned by her sudden appearance as she was by his presence. He clutched a cup of steaming coffee in his hands, a splotch of the dark brew staining the front of his shirt where it had sloshed over the lip of the mug when he'd spun around.

Good, she hoped he'd burned himself.

"What are you doing here?" she asked, not kindly, grasping for the edges of a robe that wasn't there. Instead, she was standing in the middle of her family's kitchen, covered only by the paper-thin camisole she'd worn beneath her bridesmaid gown.

Last night, after she'd dug her brother's spare house key out of the flower bed where he kept it hidden in the bottom of a resin lawn ornament and climbed the stairs to her old bedroom, she'd shrugged out of the pink-and-green concoction, but left the camisole on. With spaghetti straps and a hem that hit high on the thigh, it was no more revealing than any of her other satin nighties.

Besides, she'd been alone in the house...just her and Dom Pérignon...and not expecting guests.

"I could ask you the same thing," Connor responded, setting his mug on the countertop and grabbing a paper towel to blot at the stain on his shirt, just above the waistband of his low-slung jeans.

Lord, he wore denims like no one else she'd ever seen. Even out in L.A., where every waiter or valet was an aspiring actor or model, the men didn't have waists and hips and buttocks like Connor Riordan. They would never be able to pull off the open flannel shirts over faded T-shirts the way he did, or the worn blue jeans and work boots.

Not that it had any effect on her whatsoever. She was merely making a mental observation, the same as she might be slightly awed by a famous, high-powered celebrity who waltzed into her office back on Wilshire.

"In case you've forgotten, this is my house."

"Since when?"

She lifted a brow, her annoyance growing in direct proportion to the pounding in her skull. What she wouldn't give for a cup of that coffee and fifty aspirin right about now.

But she couldn't have those things just yet. Not until she'd finished this argument with Connor and kicked him out on his tight-but-aggravating butt.

"Since I grew up here. Remember?"

"That was a long time ago," he remarked, picking up his mug once again and taking a slow sip of the black coffee that was making her mouth water. "Seems to me it's not so much your house anymore. Your parents moved to a smaller place on the other side of town, and you moved all the way to Los Angeles. It's your brother's place now...his and Karen's."

Beth's teeth gritted together and she felt her right eye begin to twitch, which it only did when she was resisting the urge to clobber somebody.

"I'm still family," she told him, jaw clenched tight so that her words sounded half growled, even to her own ears. "This is my family home, and I'm sure Nick won't mind me staying in my old room for a few nights while he's on his honeymoon."

Like she owed him any explanation! Honestly, this was *her* house—her family home, at any rate. *He* was the interloper. *He* should be the one defending himself and offering up explanations for why he was here.

"Well, sweetheart," he drawled, "that's where we might have a problem. Because Nick told me I could stay here until he gets back."

Scowling, she let his words sink in, all the while wishing her brother were nearby so she could wring his neck. Was it too much to ask that she be allowed to stay in her childhood home while she was in Ohio? Alone. To rest and recuperate before going back to her mile-a-minute world and no-rest-for-the-weary occupation.

"Why do you need to stay here?" she wanted to know. "Don't you have a house of your own to go to?"

She could have sworn he blushed at that. His cheekbones turned a dull red and he refused to meet her gaze.

"Yeah," he said in a low rumble. "You'd think that would make a difference."

"Excuse me?"

"I got kicked out, okay?" he grumbled, crossing his arms over his chest and slouching against the counter cabinets.

He was pouting. And looking decidedly embarrassed, Beth thought.

Oh, the day was taking a turn for the better, after all.

She perked up, fighting the urge to giggle at his obvious discomfort and reversal of fortune.

"You got kicked out," she repeated, trying not to sound too gleeful. "Of your own house. Why?"

The flush disappeared from his face, then was replaced by the flat, grim line of his mouth.

"Never mind why," was his terse reply. "The point is, I needed a place to stay, and your brother offered the use of his house until he and Karen get back from their honeymoon."

It was her turn to cross her arms. At this point, she didn't even care that the gesture pushed her breasts up and caused the flimsy satin and lace bodice to bunch and reveal a fair amount of cleavage.

If the sight offended him, fine. If it turned him off, so be it. And if it turned him on... good. Maybe he would feel intimidated by his attraction to her and hightail it to the nearest hotel.

Or back into Lori-Lisa-Laura's open arms.

Okay, that didn't sit as well with her as the two previous possibilities, but still…whatever got him out of her brother's house while she was there.

"Well, you can't stay here," she told him again, more firmly this time.

"Oh, no? You want to call Nick in Hawaii, interrupt whatever he and Karen are up to at this particular moment—" he waggled his eyebrows to indicate what he predicted they'd be doing, and probably wasn't far off the mark "—and ask him exactly who his choice is for houseguest while he's gone?"

"Sure," she said, calling his bluff. "I'm pretty

sure he'll pick me, considering how I'm his *sister* and all. His blood relative."

"And I'm his best friend since fifth grade," Connor put in. "Not to mention *invited*. Does Nick even know you're here?"

"Of course he knows I'm here," she fired back.

When she'd first been making arrangements to return to Ohio for his wedding, she'd offered to get a hotel room. *Wanted* to, to be honest. But Nick had insisted she stay at the house.

"It's your house, too," he'd cajoled. "And besides, Karen and I will be leaving right after the reception. You'll have the whole place to yourself."

She'd agreed, partly because she didn't want to hurt his feelings, and partly because she'd been looking forward to coming home, sleeping in her old bedroom, and just being *alone* with her thoughts and her memories for a few days.

So much for that, she reflected now. She hadn't even been able to wake up and get a cup of coffee on only her second morning back without coming face-to-face with her greatest nemesis.

Well, part of that may be true, but she'd be damned if he'd keep her from her daily shot of caffeine a second longer.

Marching forward, she grabbed a ceramic mug from the cupboard just above Connor's right shoulder and poured herself a cup of rich, black coffee from the still-hot carafe. She crossed to the refrigerator to add a dollop of milk, then leaned back against the opposite countertop to stir in a spoonful of sugar.

She took a sip, savoring the sweet, creamy brew before Connor's voice interrupted her momentary enjoyment.

"So if Nick knows you're here, and he knows I'm here, I guess that means he thought the two of us could act like mature adults and stay together in the same house for a while without killing each other."

Beth swallowed another great gulp of coffee

before spearing him with a saccharine grin. "He'd have been wrong."

"Come on, Beth Ann." He set his coffee on the counter with a clink, sliding his thumbs into the front pockets of his jeans as he shifted to face her more fully.

She cringed at his use of both her first and middle names together, hoping he didn't notice. If he did, he would call her that all the more just to annoy her, the same as he had when they were kids.

"Can't we get along well enough to rattle around this place together for a few days? I'll stay out of your way if you stay out of mine."

I'd rather chew broken glass, she thought, downing the last of her coffee, then moving to refill her cup.

"I sincerely doubt it," she told him bluntly, not bothering to look at him. Pivoting on the ball of her bare foot, she started from the room. "I'll find somewhere else to stay."

Four

Connor watched her saunter out of the room, unable to decide whether he'd won or lost that round. Lost, would be his guess.

He should have taken the opportunity to talk to her like he'd wanted to last night. To sit down with her and discuss their relationship. That night seven years ago, when they'd done something they shouldn't have, and how it had affected them to this day.

Instead, he'd been so surprised by her sudden

appearance in the kitchen doorway that he'd let her goad him into arguing with her.

Truth be told, it had been kind of fun. She'd stood there in that frilly little excuse for a night-gown… shoulders bare, breasts heaving, bottom hem barely covering the area where he prayed panties had been.

It was too much for him to imagine her naked under there. He was already hard and throbbing just from her mere presence. Knowing she wasn't wearing underwear would have caused smoke to pour out of his ears for sure.

As it was, a cold shower and a quick dip into a subzero freezer weren't out of the question.

Her nose had been pointing up in the air, her glacial gaze implying he was no better than a piece of chewing gum she might scrape off the bottom of her steel-heeled stilettos.

She was a snob, but she hadn't always been like that. Hadn't been anything like that before college. And then he'd seduced her, taken advantage of her, and he was very much afraid he was responsible for the woman she was today.

A successful entertainment attorney, with her own firm, making more money in a year than he'd probably earn in a lifetime? Sure. But also a cold, calculating professional who put her career ahead of her family and personal happiness.

The old Beth would never have let anything come between her and her parents or brother. The new Beth had purposely moved over two thousand miles away and didn't come home unless it was absolutely unavoidable.

It was his fault she'd grown so distant from her family, but damned if he knew what to do to fix the problem.

"You've got to be kidding me."

Beth flicked mascara over her lashes while balancing the cordless phone between her ear and shoulder. The minute she'd left the kitchen and turned her back on Connor, she'd gone about trying to figure out exactly what she should do to get away from him permanently. She thought about going back downstairs and forcibly removing him from the house, but doubted she could budge his hulking, overbearing frame.

Now, she was on the phone with the airline, trying to change her flight back to L.A. So far, she was having about as much luck as she'd had trying to get a decent, quiet breakfast this morning.

Her stomach growled, sending her an uncomfortable reminder that she still hadn't eaten and was *hungry,* darn it. Which only put her more on edge.

The way she was feeling, she might just stand a decent chance of muscling Connor out of the house, after all.

"All right, if I can't get a flight out today, I'll take one for tomorrow," she told the woman on the other end of the line.

She heard the *clickety-clack* of fingers tapping

a keyboard for a second, and then the woman said, "I'm not showing anything for tomorrow, either."

"What about another airline? I don't care if it costs more. I'll even buy another ticket, I just *really* need to fly out of here as soon as possible."

Click-click-clack. "No, ma'am, I'm sorry. And I feel it's only fair to warn you that the storm front moving in has forced us to delay and cancel many of our flights. You may not even be able to get out of town with your current reservation."

Beth muttered a curse, resisting the urge to rub her eyes and smear the makeup she'd just spent the last quarter of an hour applying. She wanted to ask the woman to check the schedule again. She even thought about putting on her dragon-lady act and insisting the airline do whatever it took to get her home. But her current predicament wasn't the woman's fault, and neither was the weather.

"All right, thank you," she forced herself to say in a polite, moderate tone before hanging up.

No flights. Not today, tomorrow…maybe not for the rest of the week. This definitely put a crimp in her plans, but she hadn't gotten where she was in this world by taking no for an answer.

The bathroom door opened with a creak of hinges, and she crossed the hall to her childhood bedroom, where her suitcase lay open on top of the unmade bed. She slipped her stockinged feet into the basic black sling-backs she'd brought to go along with most of the outfits she'd packed and headed downstairs to find a phone book.

She didn't know where Connor was, and told herself she didn't care. It was too much to hope that he might have abandoned the house of his own free will, but maybe if she could avoid him for another few minutes, things would work out okay.

Keeping her ears open for signs that he was moving around the house, she crept into the room her brother used as an office-slash-den and started rooting around. She found the phone book in a drawer beneath the phone. So sensible, it had to be Karen's doing. Nick didn't have an organized bone in his body and was as likely to leave the phone book in the dishwasher as the office.

She dropped into the chair behind the desk and flipped to the lodgings section at the back of the directory. There were any number of two- and three-star motels listed, as well as a couple of decent hotels. She would have to drive an hour or more to find a really nice place to stay, but at this point she would be happy with just a bed and private bathroom.

The telephone receiver was in her hand, her fingers tapping out the first of the hotel numbers, when she suddenly froze.

What was she doing? Why was she the one calling the airline and trying to find another place to stay when this was *her* house?

Well, her brother's house now, but she'd lived

here with him and their parents for the first twenty years of her life. That certainly had to count for more than Connor's close friendship with Nick and the fact that he'd lived across the street from them for almost the same amount of time.

Dropping the phone back in its cradle, she slapped the directory closed and stood, sending the chair scuttling back several inches.

No, she wasn't going to do this. She was going to stay in her own house, in her own room, until she flew back to Los Angeles.

Hopefully that would be Thursday, on her original ticket. But if the weather grounded that flight, she would stay until the next one available to the West Coast.

It wouldn't be the most comfortable few days she'd ever spent, she knew. Being in the same town with Connor was difficult enough…staying in the same house with him was bound to give her a migraine of epic proportions.

No problem; she'd brought her Imitrex. Along

with plain ibuprofen, antacids and all the other over-the-counter medications she kept on hand for when her body began to protest the long hours and high stress levels she forced it to endure.

The point was, she'd been telling herself for years that she was well and truly over Connor. No more childhood crush, no more unrealistic, adolescent fantasies that he couldn't fulfill. Now was the time to step up and prove it.

She was debating her plan of action where Connor was concerned when he poked his head around the doorway, startling her. For a nano-second, her heart stopped beating as it jumped into her throat.

"You're still here," he said unnecessarily.

"Yes." She drew herself up, smoothing the front of her white silk blouse, though she doubted she'd picked up any wrinkles in the short amount of time she'd been dressed. "And I'm staying, so you might want to look into finding other accommodations."

"What's the matter? Couldn't get an earlier flight?"

His eyes twinkled devilishly and her jaw snapped closed. He was so aggravating, the way he seemed to know what she was thinking and find it amusing.

"No, actually. There's a storm front moving in, and they're not sure I'll even be able to leave at the scheduled time."

"You could always go to a hotel," he offered, moving to fill the doorway and leaning a shoulder against the carved-wood jamb.

"So could you."

"Stalemate, then. Since we've been down this road before, and neither of us is willing to leave, I guess that means we're stuck together."

She hated to admit it, but he was right. They were well and truly stuck with each other.

"Come on." Connor pushed away from the wall and motioned toward the kitchen with a hitch of his head. "If we're going to be roommates for a while, we might as well make nice. I fixed breakfast. Come get some."

With that, he turned and walked away, leaving her to follow or not. She stood behind the desk for another minute, debating whether to let down her guard and eat with him or hold tight to her pride and avoid him as much as possible.

A whiff of toast and other unidentifiable scents floated into the room, causing her stomach to rumble and making up her mind for her. She was starving, he'd cooked, and she'd be darned if he'd keep her from eating when she was hungry in her own home.

She crossed the office and strolled down the hall, her high heels clicking in cadence with her steps. When she reached the kitchen, she found Connor at the stove, stirring something in a frying pan and scooping portions onto plates.

As though sensing her presence, he glanced in her direction, then carried the two heaping plates to the table.

"Have a seat," he told her. "I'll get the toast and some napkins."

Waiting until he was back at the counter, she skirted him and settled in the chair nearest the wall. That way, she could see every move he made and map out her escape route, if one became necessary.

He piled four slices of buttered toast on another plate and grabbed a handful of paper napkins from a drawer by the sink before returning to the table.

"Don't wait for me. Go ahead and eat."

She lifted the fork at her place setting, but merely toyed with the omelet fixings in front of her while he continued to move around the room. He opened a cupboard and retrieved two glasses, taking them with him to the refrigerator.

"Milk or juice?" he asked.

Juice would go better with breakfast, but her ulcer wouldn't thank her for it. "Milk. Thank you," she added grudgingly.

After filling the glasses—one with milk for her, the other with orange juice for himself—he sauntered back to the table with that confident, loose-limbed stride of his, kicked his chair out and took a seat.

"How's your omelet?"

She looked down, realizing she hadn't yet tasted a bite.

"Oh." Quickly, she scooped up a forkful of ham, cheese, onion, mushroom and pepper, mixed in with scrambled egg. Her personal trainer would kill her if he ever found out she'd eaten like this, but she had to admit it was delicious.

Of course, she wasn't going to tell Connor that.

"It's very good," she told him, dabbing the corners of her mouth with her napkin.

"Glad you like it." He dug into his own breakfast like a man who hadn't eaten in a week.

She picked at hers more slowly, feeling the silence growing between them like a weight on her chest.

"I didn't know you cooked," she murmured, when she couldn't stand it any longer.

After taking a swig of orange juice, he shook his head. "I don't much. Just enough to get by."

"I suppose Lori-Laura-Lisa does most of the cooking for you these days." The words sounded bitter, even to her own ears, and Beth regretted voicing them as soon as they passed her lips.

"Lori-Laura-Lisa?" he asked, one brow quirking upward.

She shrugged, refusing to be embarrassed by either her comment or the grouping of names she used for his overly processed girlfriend. "I know it starts with an *L*."

"*Lori,*" he emphasized. "Her name is Lori. And she cooks some, but mostly we go out or order in. How about you? What do you eat out there in L.A.?"

"Not eggs and ham, that's for sure," she said, stabbing at those very ingredients on her plate and relaxing into the conversation. "Tofu, protein shakes, salads. A lot of raw meals."

"Raw?" he wanted to know, wiggling his eyebrows suggestively.

Against her better judgment, Beth found herself smiling at his lighthearted teasing. "Not that kind of raw. Get your mind out of the gutter, pervert," she fired back.

He only grinned and shoveled another pile of omelet into his mouth.

"Raw is a big thing out on the coast. Uncooked, unpreserved, organic foods, like chickpea burgers with shredded coconut or carrots on top."

"Uh-huh. And this keeps you alive?"

"I'm here, aren't I?"

"Yeah, but it wouldn't hurt you to wolf down a real burger or two before you head back. You could stand to put on a couple pounds."

Something warm and pleasant burst low in her solar plexus. She spent so much time working out and watching what she ate, trying hard to fit in with the "the skinnier the better" California mentality. It was an ideal she'd embraced when she'd first moved out there, but now it seemed to be a constant struggle just to maintain her current weight and figure.

Hearing Connor say she was too thin flattered her, even if it shouldn't. He didn't get an opinion about her physical appearance—no man did— and he didn't have a clue what life in L.A. was like.

But after seeing his dress-up-doll girlfriend, knowing that he didn't think she had to maintain a perfect image made her feel somehow normal and accepted. A far cry from her recent frame of mind.

"Red meat is strictly *verboten,*" she said. "And I work out two hours, three days a week to stay just this size, thank you very much."

"I hate to break it to you, sweetheart, but you're eating meat right now."

She looked down at the specks of pink cooked into fluffy clouds of yellow egg. "Yes, well, technically ham isn't red meat, and while I wouldn't normally eat it, I thought it would be rude to turn down your offer of breakfast. Besides, it's not much and there are other, healthier things in here, like onions and peppers."

"Excellent job of justifying."

She shot him a cheeky twist of her lips. "Thank you." He didn't need to know just how well versed she was at the justification game.

"You're welcome to go running after you eat, if you want. Burn off all those nasty calories."

"I just might." But a sidelong glance out the kitchen window told her she wouldn't want to. The day was looking decidedly overcast, and the wind was whipping the leaves around on the trees.

"Actually…" Connor stopped to clear his throat.

He stared down at the table rather than meet her gaze, and a slick, uncomfortable sensation snaked over Beth's skin.

"I was kind of hoping we could talk after breakfast."

Her heart kicked up its pace, sending the blood racing through her veins, and the slick feeling turned to a cool clamminess.

Honestly, she had no idea why Connor was so determined to speak with her. He'd tried to drag her off last night at the reception so they could talk, and now he was making a second attempt to get her to listen to whatever he had to say.

The queasiness in her stomach, though, told her she didn't want to hear it. Or maybe she was just afraid that he'd bring up the past, tearing open a wound long ago healed over.

After all, what else did they have to discuss? They hadn't seen each other, except briefly, in the last seven years.

She swallowed hard, taking a minute to get her thoughts and jumbled emotions in order before forcing herself to respond. "What do we have to talk about?"

He tossed his crumpled-up napkin on top of his now-empty plate and pushed them away from him. Crossing his arms in front of him on the table, he lifted his head and met her eyes with his own, which looked like two chips of brittle brown ice.

His voice rang low but clear as he drawled, "That night."

The words drove into her like bullets and for a moment, she couldn't breathe, even though she'd known exactly what was coming.

Why did he have to bring it up? Why now, after all these years? Why at all?

It had been a mistake, but it had happened. She'd gotten on with her life, and so, obviously, had he.

"What night?" she asked, playing dumb while her brain struggled to regain its equilibrium.

"You know what night, Beth. We both do. That night after the football game, in my truck."

She laughed lightly, doing her best to act nonchalant while her insides continued to quake. "Goodness, why would you bring that up after all these years? It was aeons ago. I would have thought you'd forgotten all about it. I certainly had."

A beat passed while he seemed to absorb her comment, and then his gaze grew shuttered, his mouth thinning into a flat, pale line.

"I'm sorry to hear that. It's something I think about all the time."

She didn't know what to do with that piece of information. Be flattered, angry, curious?

At the moment, she mostly felt cold. He thought about that night all the time, but he hadn't thought enough of her, or of what had passed between them, to pick up the phone and call her afterward. The next day, the next week…she'd have taken anything, any small sign that he was still interested in her.

Even a face-to-face meeting where he sat her down and told her he wasn't interested and didn't want to see her again would have been better than nothing. But he hadn't even had the courtesy to do that, so instead they'd spent nearly a decade flitting around each other, avoiding, pretending, denying anything had ever happened between them.

And now…well, she had no interest in allowing him to bring all those stinging memories and emotions bubbling to the surface again. He'd had his chance to make peace seven years ago; she wasn't willing to give him a fresh opportunity now.

Falling back on her day-to-day, all-business persona, she pushed her chair away from the table and stood, her posture yardstick straight, her movements quick and precise.

"Why are you bringing this up after so long?" she asked, carrying her empty plate and glass to the sink. Then she backtracked and did the same with his dishes.

He turned in his seat to face her, the wood creaking beneath his weight, and propped one arm on the table. "Because we never discussed it before, and it's obviously putting a strain on our relationship."

"We don't have a relationship," she said with a sharp bark of laughter.

For once, she was almost finding this situation amusing. It was the height of irony that Connor suddenly seemed so determined to discuss the state of affairs between them when she'd spent every single one of her teenage years praying for Connor to play a larger part in her life.

"Sure we do, Beth."

She was leaning back against the counter by the sink, her arms up, the heels of her hands propped along the sharp edge at her waistline. When he rose to his feet and stalked toward her, her fingers tightened reflexively on the cool Formica, but she refused to move, refused to flinch or in any other way reveal her discomfort.

Her entire stay in this house with him was going to be an exercise in discomfort, so she might as well get used to it right now and learn to school her features, reactions and body language.

"Everyone in this world has a relationship with everyone else, from married couples to the cashiers and customers down at the Qwik Fill. You're my best friend's sister, practically family—of course we have a relationship. I wasn't implying we were any more intimately involved than that."

"Good," was the best response she could come up with. Her lungs refused to expand and deflate normally, his nearness sucking all the oxygen out of the air around them.

"But we were once, weren't we?" he murmured in a low voice.

The metal edge of the countertop dug into the soft cushion of her palms and she concentrated on that sharp throb of sensation to block the flood of memories threatening to spill into her brain. She would not go back to that time. She wouldn't open herself up to that again, especially with him.

He was standing less than a foot away, his tall form towering over her. A faded forest-green T-shirt clung to the smooth, firm expanse of his chest, partially covered by an open blue-and-white-plaid flannel work shirt.

So informal, so blue collar… Considering the well-dressed businessmen and celebrities she worked with on a daily basis, it amazed her that she could still find his taste in clothing attractive.

After catching her breath and feeling steady enough to answer, she told him, "Once, Connor, a very long time ago. Don't make more of it than it was."

"I won't, if you won't, but that doesn't explain why you've been avoiding me all these years."

Five

"I haven't been avoiding you."

Her voice was firm, but the slight flicker in her gaze told him she was lying. Not that he needed the added assurance. It didn't take a rocket scientist to figure out that when one person entered a room and another either made an excuse to leave or simply slipped away unnoticed, something was going on.

Not that he blamed her. He'd acted like an ass all those years ago. Yes, he'd been twenty-six and thought he was grown-up and mature, but he'd handled the entire situation badly.

To start, he'd taken advantage of a twenty-one-year-old Beth. His hormones had gotten the better of him and he'd given in to raging, long-repressed desires that would have been better off remaining repressed. He wasn't sure he could ever forgive himself for that. It ate at him like a wasting disease.

Then what had he done? He'd dropped her off at her house and never spoken to her again. Well, not never, but barely. He hadn't phoned her the next day to see if she was okay, or swung by to talk to her about how their having sex might have changed things between them.

No, he'd taken the coward's way out and stayed away until he knew she was back at school. And then he'd continued skulking around with his tail tucked under, content to keep his mouth shut on the topic for as long as she was.

But that plan had backfired on him, hadn't it?

Not discussing it hadn't made the situation go away or allowed their relationship to settle back to normal. Instead, it had turned the incident into a boil that festered and grew not only ugly, but painful.

They'd drifted apart when they used to be so close. They avoided each other, when they used to seek one another out. They couldn't even make eye contact without one or the other of them quickly looking away. And there were no more smiles, no more teasing, no more inside childhood jokes.

He hated that. He hated that his overactive libido and lack of control had caused Beth to throw up a barrier between them as thick and tall as the Great Wall of China.

And once again, he wasn't making great strides at setting things right.

What was it about Beth that put all of his senses on high alert and made him want to push, prod, draw her out?

For better or worse, he wanted to get her to react. Yell at him, scream at him, slap him silly. Cry, laugh, or throw herself into his arms. At this point, he'd take just about anything. Any sign that she wasn't as indifferent toward him as she claimed.

"No?" he put in, in response to her assertion. "What would you call seven years of circling each other like opposing magnets?"

"I don't know what you're talking about."

"Sure you do. It used to be that I'd come over and you'd race downstairs to see me. You'd beg me to stay and watch a movie or drive you to the store for the latest teen magazine. And then there was that night in my truck. After that, any time I came over while you were home, you made yourself scarce. You even moved all the way out to California so you'd have an excuse not to visit very often."

She gave a small huff of laughter that never reached her eyes. "That's ridiculous. I moved to California because I wanted to be an entertainment lawyer, and that's the entertainment capital of the world."

"Did you?" He took a single step closer with the question. "Or did you decide to become an entertainment attorney because it was the one type of law you couldn't practice here at home?"

This time, she didn't laugh. She didn't even scoff at his accusation.

Her arms fell from where they'd been propped against the edge of the counter and took up stiff residence across her chest. Little did she know the gesture lifted her breasts and caused the airy silk of her white blouse to separate just above her cleavage, allowing him a clear view of full, fleshy hills and the deep, shadowed valley between.

The sight made his mouth go dry, but he didn't look for long, for fear she'd catch him staring.

"I'm good at what I do, Connor, and I like living in L.A. Not that I have to justify anything to you."

She was right, of course, but that didn't keep him from being curious.

"Now, if you're finished bringing up incidents from the past that have no relevance to the present and giving me the third degree, I think it's about time we establish some ground rules for however long we'll be forced to stay here together."

"Ground rules, huh?" He crossed his arms, mimicking her defensive stance, even though he was fighting back amusement. "What do you have in mind?"

"For one thing, I get first dibs on the bathroom in the morning."

"How do you figure?"

"It's my brother's house, and I'm the girl," she remarked, deadpan.

He had to bite the inside of his mouth to keep from hooting with laughter.

"You're the girl? Is that a defense that would stand up in court?"

"I don't spend a lot of time in court, so I

wouldn't know, but the fact remains that women need more time in the bathroom in the mornings."

Having lived with Lori for the past three years, that was something he knew quite well. "I agree, but there's one small problem with your plan."

"What?"

"I was up a good hour earlier than you were this morning. Do you expect me to wait to use the john just because you're supposed to get first dibs?"

Her lips turned down in a frown, her nose wrinkling only slightly at his frank terminology.

"Fine. If you're up before I am, then you can use the bathroom. But as soon as I'm awake, my needs take precedence."

"Deal. Anything else?"

"Meals. You cooked breakfast this morning, and I appreciate it. It was very good, thank you. But don't feel that you have to do the same every morning, or for any other meals. And don't expect me to cook, either. I say it's every man for himself. If one of us cooks and wants to invite the other to share the meal, fine. But neither of us should expect the other to feed them."

"Fine. How about takeout? Do we confer with each other before calling for pizza or Chinese, or do we treat it like a covert mission?"

"Very funny," she smirked. "That's your call. It might be polite to let each other know if we're calling out for food, but it isn't required."

"Got it. Anything else?"

Several seconds ticked by while she considered, and then she shook her head. "I can't think of anything more at the moment, but we can tack on new rules as they come up."

"Fine by me." He let his arms slip down and planted his hands halfway inside his front jeans pockets.

"So who does the dishes?" he wanted to know, tilting his head toward the dirty ones in the sink behind her.

"You do," she said without batting an

eyelash, then turned on her heel and sashayed out of the kitchen.

Connor watched her go, enjoying the sassy, well-dressed view. As soon as she disappeared around the corner, he chuckled, turning to the sink and running water for the dishes he was apparently expected to clean for as long as they were staying in the same house together.

Since she was going to be stuck in Crystal Springs for a few days, anyway, Beth decided to call some of her old friends and touch base. Most of her high-school girlfriends had drifted away, but there were still a few she kept in touch with, a few still living in town.

She was embarrassed to admit it, but she'd nearly let them slip away, too. The occasional phone call when she wasn't working late, or a quickly scrawled note that she then asked her assistant to mail was about the extent of her contact with Jackie and Gail these past few years. And more often than not, those instances were prompted only by a friendly, if nosy, reminder from her mother.

Thankfully, neither of her friends seemed to hold it against her. Both were as giddy and upbeat as ever when she called, and wasted no time in talking her into going out with them to the Longneck, Crystal Springs's local watering hole, on Wednesday night.

She hadn't been out just for fun in years, probably since she'd moved to L.A. There were bars and clubs aplenty out there, of course, but it seemed that any time she got the chance to frequent them, it was for business purposes. Wooing prospective, high-profile clients or meeting with current, equally high-profile ones at a place of their choosing.

The only problem was that she needed a ride. Jackie worked part-time as a receptionist at a local medical clinic and was the mother of four, two still in diapers. Beth knew from previous conversations with her friend that their family's only car was a mess of toys, fast-food containers and diaper-bag supplies. So even if Jackie's husband hadn't needed the car that evening, she was in no hurry to ride around in a vehicle that smelled like sour milk and old French fries.

And Gail, who was married with no children, worked until seven in the evening. She'd insisted it was no problem to swing by and pick up both Jackie and Beth after she'd run home for a shower and change of clothes, but that would have meant not meeting at the Longneck until nine, which would keep them there probably well past midnight, which was too late for Jackie to be away from her kids.

All in all, it would just be easier for Beth to find her own ride.

She thought about renting a car, since it wasn't a bad idea to have transportation of her own while she was home. But the nearest car-rental agency was in the next big town over, forty-five minutes away. So whatever she decided, she'd still need a ride.

It pained her to do it, but she would have to ask Connor to drive her into town Wednesday night. After the way they'd parted company this morning, that would be about as much fun as hanging cinder blocks from her eyelids.

Leaving the office, she headed for the kitchen, thinking she might find him there. But the kitchen was empty, clean breakfast dishes propped and drying in the drainer beside the sink.

She smiled at that, remembering how she'd left them for him. It had been a truly beautiful moment... the flash of stunned disbelief that crossed his face and the fact that she'd been able to get in the last word of their highly charged exchange.

Too bad she was about to lose the upper hand by groveling for a ride into town.

She checked the living room next, and then the dining room, but the whole downstairs was empty. Maybe he was in Nick's room, which he was using as his own.

He'd better not be asleep or in any form of undress. She'd wait to ask him about the ride, if that was the case.

Climbing the stairs, she walked down the short hallway and tapped on her brother's open bedroom door. From what she could see, the bed was made, the blinds on the single window were open, and the only sign of Connor's residence was an open duffel on the floor by the dresser. He'd apparently gone home to his own house at some point to collect a few personal items and changes of clothes.

"Connor?" she called out when he didn't respond to her knock.

She was turning, planning to go back downstairs and see if his truck was even in the driveway, when she heard his muffled voice.

"Connor?"

"Yeah, in here," he repeated more loudly.

It sounded as if he was in Nick's old room—the one he'd occupied all through childhood, until their parents had moved to an apartment in a residential village across town. Karen had moved in with him then, and they'd taken over the master bedroom.

She turned the knob and pushed open the door, not knowing what to expect.

Connor stood on the far side of the room, holding a large cardboard box with Nick's Trophies written on the side in black Magic Marker. He dropped the box on a pile of others and turned to face her as she stepped into the room.

"Hi," he said, wiping his hands on the side of his pants.

"Hi. What are you doing in here?"

"Do you know if Nick and Karen have any plans for this room?" he asked, neatly avoiding her question.

She glanced around, taking in the plain, fawn-colored walls, complete with pinpricks from where Nick had tacked up dozens of posters, and the threadbare gray carpeting that had been there when her parents moved in more than thirty-five years before.

"No, I have no idea. Why?"

"Because it would make a great nursery, don't you think?"

His comment caught her off guard. The room had been used for storage for so long, and had belonged to a teenage boy for a decade before that. It might be smarter to burn it down and start from scratch.

"I don't know, it looks a little grimy in here." She wrinkled her nose. "And it smells."

Connor chuckled. "Nick's sweaty old gym socks, no doubt. But that should be easy enough to take care of. Seriously," he said, shifting to stand by her side, shoulder to shoulder, facing the room. "Pull up the carpeting, slap on a fresh coat of paint, stick some pastel curtains on the windows, and fill the room with baby furniture… I'd say they'd have themselves a nursery."

He turned his head, meeting her gaze. "Wouldn't it be a great welcome-home present for them?"

"And who's going to do all this marvelous re-decorating?" she wanted to know.

His mouth curved upward in a cocky grin. "You forget who you're talking to, sweetheart. Your brother and I are partners in our own con-tracting company, and we work the jobs our-selves ninety-five percent of the time, right along with our crews. I can have the floor stripped and refinished in no time. And how long could it take to paint four small walls?"

He nudged her in the ribs with his elbow. "Come on, have some faith. What do you say?"

Her brother and new sister-in-law would be de-lighted, she had no doubt about that. They would need a nursery eventually, anyway, and this way they wouldn't have to do any of the work.

With a small shrug, she said, "Do whatever you want. I'm sure Nick and Karen will appreciate it."

She started to turn, only to have Connor grab her arm, holding her in place. The warmth of his wide, full fingertips soaked straight through the silk of her blouse, heating her skin and thinning her blood.

"Wait." When she returned her attention to his face, he continued. "I thought maybe you could help."

Oh, no. That was too much to ask, too much to bear.

If he wanted to rip the room apart and rebuild, repaint, remodel, it was his business. His carpentry skills were excellent, so she felt confident he wouldn't leave the room in shambles.

But she wanted nothing to do with it. Truth be told, she didn't even particularly want to know a nursery was being designed anywhere near her.

"I'd rather not," she said, lacing her arms across her chest in a protective gesture. Already she felt chilled, goose bumps rising along her arms and neck.

"Why not? You'd be great. You could help me pick out paint colors, curtains, border paper. Not to mention the crib, changing table, that sort of thing. I'm clueless about baby stuff."

And she was supposed to be so much more knowledgeable?

A stab of pain hit her low in the belly. She bit her lip to keep a moan from climbing its way up her throat and blinked her suddenly damp eyes.

"Don't you have to work this week?" she asked instead, hoping to divert his attention from how pale she knew her face must be.

"On and off, yeah, but this is a slow time of year for us. Nick wouldn't have agreed to take a two-week honeymoon if it weren't. Most of the deals we have going now are inside jobs, and our men can handle the work in my place for a few days. That's the beauty of owning your own company," he added with a self-assured smile.

Seconds ticked by so slowly, they felt like hours. Her head ached. Her ears buzzed. If he hadn't been holding her arm, she feared she might have fallen over.

"I really need your help, Beth. I'm not sure I can do this without you, and I want to have it done before Nick and Karen come home."

Something in his eyes seeped past her resistance. She didn't want to be involved. *Oh,* how she didn't want to be involved. But it would mean the world to Nick and Karen, Connor was right about that. And she was going to be an aunt soon. It was time to start getting used to the idea of being around a baby, whether she liked it or not.

Swallowing hard, she nodded. Her voice sounded rusty, but she forced the words past her dry lips. "All right. I guess I don't have anything better to do while I'm in town, anyway."

He didn't seem to take offense at her answer, even though she'd been half hoping he would. A nice ugly argument was exactly what she needed to drive away cold and painful memories.

Instead, his expression brightened and he gave her a quick hug. Not enough to get her hackles up, but a light, friendly embrace to say thanks.

"The hardware store is closed on Sundays, and everywhere else will be closing soon, too, so we might as well wait until tomorrow to go shopping for supplies. I'll start making a list right now. Wanna help?"

She shook her head. At the moment, she needed to be alone. She needed a drink and a hot bath and an hour or two to get her mind back on the present rather than wallowing in the past.

"You go ahead. I can add to it tomorrow if I think of anything you've missed."

"Sounds good." He gave her arm one last squeeze before heading out of the room.

"Oh, Connor," she said, stopping him before he could disappear down the hall.

"Yeah?"

She cleared her throat before saying more, not wanting him to hear the emotion in her voice. "Some friends of mine want to get together at the Longneck Wednesday night. Since I don't have a car, while I'm in town, I was wondering if you'd mind driving me. If it's too much trouble," she hurried on, "don't worry about it. I can always bum a ride from someone else, or rent a car between now and then."

She'd already thought through both of those ideas and knew they weren't going to be the least convenient, but if he had other plans, she could do it.

"No problem," he said with a shake of his head. Hitching his thumb into his front jeans pocket, he shot her a brief smile. "I haven't been to the Longneck in a while myself. It might be nice to go in to have a drink and catch up. Just let me know what time you want to leave, okay?"

She made her head move up and down in agreement, and after a moment, he left.

Beth stood where she was for several minutes, fighting back tears.

That hadn't been as hard as she'd expected, not after the punch to the gut he'd given her by asking her to help fix up and decorate a nursery.

She never should have come home. She *knew* it would be this way, *knew* bad memories and old wounds would be brought to the surface.

If only she'd gotten out of town right after the reception instead of agreeing to stay a few extra days to please her parents. If only she'd left the house as soon as she realized Connor would be staying here, too. Sleeping on the street would have been preferable to dealing with this deep, throbbing ache that seemed to take over her entire body.

And she had only herself to blame.

Beth waited until Connor was stretched out on the couch, feet propped on the coffee table, list of supplies on his lap while he sipped a beer and watched something on the sports channel, to sneak into the kitchen for a bottle of wine.

Tiptoeing back upstairs, she shut herself into the bathroom and started drawing a bath. She poured a generous amount of bubble bath into the stream of roaring water and then started to undress as the small room filled with the scent of lavender.

Once she was nude, she poured a glass of the rich red claret, set it on the rim of the tub, leaving the bottle within reach, and stepped inside the foaming, steaming water.

Ah, heaven, she thought as she turned off the water and slipped beneath its heady spell. A good bubble bath went a long way toward curing life's ills.

Unfortunately, it didn't go quite far enough tonight. She would need a lot more bubbles and a lot more wine to block out the memories her latest encounter with Connor had stirred up.

No. She wasn't going to think about that. Not

anymore, not right now. This time was for healing, forgetting.

Taking another drink of wine, she leaned her head back against the edge of the tub, closed her eyes and tried to think of anything other than what weighed heaviest on her heart.

She thought about her brother's wedding, and how happy he and Karen had both looked while saying their vows. She thought about her parents' excited faces each time she stepped off the plane after being away for so long, often more than a year.

She thought about all the work that awaited when she got back to Los Angeles. Contracts to go over, phone calls to return, and likely a few high-strung celebrities to calm down.

The more her mind wandered to work issues, the sleepier she got, until her muscles began to relax and she could feel herself starting to fall asleep.

And then the funniest thing happened. Just before she drifted off completely, Connor's face played across her subconscious and pulled the lid right off of everything she'd been fighting so hard to keep under wraps.

Six

She was twenty-one again and a senior in college—old enough to drink but young enough to still feel carefree and invincible.

Most importantly, though, she was in love. And finally, after so many years of wishing and dreaming, she was pretty sure he was in love with her, too.

She'd gone home to Crystal Springs for the weekend, to visit her parents, and ended up going to a hometown football game with them, her brother and Connor. Afterward, she and

Connor had gone off by themselves and ended up making love. Her first time and in the cab of his pickup, but as far as she was concerned, it had been absolutely perfect.

She'd been smiling ever since. Even her friends at school had noticed and asked her about it, pressuring her for details.

But she wouldn't tell them, at least not yet. The entire experience was too new to her. Too special. Too private. It was something that only she and Connor shared, and she wanted to keep it that way a while longer.

A few days after she'd returned to school from her weekend home, though, her happiness began to fade. She'd expected Connor to call, but he hadn't.

The next time she phoned her parents, she'd even asked to talk to her brother and tried to subtly feel him out about his best friend. Had they seen each other or talked since she'd been home? Had Connor mentioned her at all? But her brother didn't seem to know anything and she hadn't wanted him to grow suspicious.

Connor would call; she was just too giddy and anxious to hear from him. In another day or two, he would call.

But the days passed, turning into weeks, and she never heard from him. Not a phone call, not an e-mail, not a short message passed to her through her family. Nothing.

And then she started getting sick. She didn't think much of it at first. A flu bug was going around campus and everyone seemed to be catching it, so she wasn't surprised when she started feeling ill like many of her friends.

Until her virus wouldn't seem to go away. Everyone else got better, but she still felt terrible. She also noticed that she was sick every morning, but started to feel better by the afternoon. By the time she realized she'd missed a period, she was already pretty sure she knew what was wrong.

She was pregnant.

With Connor's baby.

At first she was petrified. She was in her last year of law school...how was she ever going to reach graduation and be able to practice law when she was hugely pregnant or caring for a newborn? How would she tell Connor? What would her parents say when they found out?

So many thoughts and fears raced through her head, jumbling together until her nausea grew.

But what if motherhood was wonderful? What if Connor was delighted that he was going to be a father and proposed on the spot?

They could marry and move into a small house in Crystal Springs. She could do her best to finish school before the baby was born and worry about finding a job at a local law firm later.

The situation might not be ideal, but it could work. And her greatest ambition had always been to marry Connor and have a family with him...so what if they were starting a little early and doing things out of order?

Yes, everything would work out just fine. She would make plans to get home again soon and tell Connor in person.

Then, too, he could explain to her why he hadn't called since the night they spent together up at Makeout Point. She was sure he had a logical explanation and hadn't simply been ignoring her.

That thought kept her spirits up for the next two weeks while she struggled through the first month of pregnancy without letting anyone know what was really going on. It wasn't easy to keep her condition a secret, especially from her roommate, but she managed.

She was getting dressed for class one morning when the cramping began. The sensation was so dull and passed so quickly that she didn't think much of it. An hour later, though, after she'd returned from class, the cramping was much worse, and she knew something was seriously wrong. She went to the bathroom, only to find blood spotting her panties.

At that point, she didn't care who knew about her pregnancy. In tears, she'd gone to her roommate and begged her to help her get to the hospital.

But it was too late. She'd lost the baby.

She cried for weeks afterward. Her grades started to slip because of so many missed classes and exams, but no matter what her friends said or did to try to help her snap out of her depression, she remained inconsolable.

Not only that, but she began to harbor a deep resentment toward Connor, who she blamed for everything she'd been through.

He'd taken her virginity without a backward glance and left her to deal with the repercussions on her own. They'd known each other nearly all their lives, but she hadn't even warranted a phone call after they'd slept together.

Had he even once considered that she might get pregnant and need his support? Of course not. Typical man—out for his own pleasure and to hell with the consequences.

And even though she hadn't gotten the chance to tell him about the baby, she blamed him for the miscarriage, too. If he'd called or driven up to the university to visit even once after they'd had sex, he would have known and they could have begun making plans together.

She might have moved back home with him and not had to keep to a hectic class schedule that wore her out and increased her stress level. Or he might have been with her when the first cramp hit and driven her to the doctor in time for the baby to be saved. Either way, she felt certain that the situation would have turned out differently if he had made any effort to contact her after their night together.

Even if she had still lost the baby, they could

have grieved together, healed together, made plans to have another baby somewhere down the road.

Instead, she was alone and hurting, and it was all Connor's fault.

A sharp rap on the door jarred her awake. She sat up with a jerk, sending now-cool, bubbleless water sloshing over the edge of the tub.

Her face, she realized, was streaked with tears. Even in her sleep, she'd grieved for the child she'd lost all those years ago.

"Beth, you okay in there?"

Connor's voice permeated her still-sluggish brain, adding the residual emotions causing her heart to ache. A wounded moan trembled from her lips and she covered her mouth to keep from being heard.

Pushing to her feet, she grabbed a towel from the rack on the wall and wrapped it around her naked torso. Rivulets of water sluiced down her skin, dripping onto the mat on the floor as she quickly patted herself dry.

"Beth?"

"Yes, I'm fine," she called out, embarrassed to be caught sleeping, dreaming, sobbing in the tub.

"You've been in there for quite a while, and I heard you cry out. Are you sure you're all right?"

Making sure to dry her face and remove any sign that she'd been weeping, she tucked the ends of the towel above her breasts and opened the bathroom door a crack. She made herself give him a small smile as their gazes met.

"I'm fine, Connor, really. I must have dozed off in the tub."

"You look a little pale," he pointed out, studying her from head to toe as much as he could through the narrow opening.

"I've been sitting in cold water too long, I guess," she said with forced cheerfulness. "I'm all pruny."

His eyes went dark at that, his lips thinning slightly.

"If you're sure you're okay…"

"I am, thank you. I'll be out in just a minute, in case you need to use the bathroom."

"No, I'm good," he said in a low tone. "I was just worried about you."

She didn't know what to say to that, and was afraid she wouldn't be able to speak past the lump growing in her throat, so she merely nodded with downcast eyes and closed the bathroom door with a click.

Ten minutes later, she emerged with her hair freshly combed, wearing a short satin night-gown with matching sunflower yellow robe. Her feet were bare as she padded down the hardwood hallway and stairs, wineglass and bottle in hand.

Surprisingly, she was feeling better than when she'd first been startled awake from her dream…or maybe it had been more of a series of relived memories. Lord knew it was all true and had happened to her seven years before.

She tried not to think about those times any more than she had to, but being home and so near Connor muddied the waters and made it almost impossible to deny the past.

Still, it had been nice of Connor to check on her, to be worried about her. And for once, she hadn't snapped at him or thrown up her ice-princess veneer.

Being in Crystal Springs again reminded her of the kind, innocent girl she used to be. She hadn't had much of a chance to be either kind or innocent lately. Polite, civil, professional… but not naturally, sincerely, down-home pleasant.

Detouring through the kitchen, she retrieved a second wineglass, then headed for the living room, where Connor was once again propped on the couch watching television.

She wasn't sure why she felt compelled to

talk with him. She could just as easily have gone to her room and avoided him until morning. But for once, her dreams or memories or whatever they were about the pregnancy and miscarriage didn't make her hate him more. For the first time, it occurred to her that she'd piled an awful lot of blame at his feet.

Yes, he'd gotten her pregnant. Yes, he'd failed to call afterward, which she still thought he should have done. But in the same vein, she could have just as easily called him—and should have after she realized that their night together had resulted in a baby.

And because he hadn't known, he really didn't bear any responsibility for the loss of that baby or for the roller-coaster ride her emotions took because of it.

She wasn't ready to tell him about the pregnancy and miscarriage…not now, maybe not ever…but it wouldn't hurt to sit and talk with him a bit. She hadn't exactly been Sister Mary

Sunshine since they'd gotten stuck together in her brother's house.

He watched her cross the carpeted floor with hooded eyes, but to his credit, his gaze never wandered to her legs, bare from a little above midthigh down. As she took a seat on the sofa beside him, setting the long-stemmed glasses on the low coffee table, he sat up and cleared his throat.

"So what do you think—pizza for supper? I was just going to call one in."

She nodded, pouring them each a healthy portion of wine. "Sounds good to me."

Pushing himself up from the couch, he set his beer aside and sauntered to the phone. Her mood was just generous enough that she watched him walking away and appreciated the view. My, he really did fill out a pair of jeans nicely.

He dialed the local pizza place and ordered a large pie, then covered the mouthpiece and asked, "I'm getting the works on my half, what do you want on yours?"

She shouldn't, but she said, "The same." She'd make up for it later…maybe get up early in the morning and go running, regardless of the weather.

"Make that one large with everything," he told the person on the other end, then gave his name and directions to the house.

Once that was done, he moved back to the sofa and reached for his beer, but she handed him a glass of wine instead.

He eyed her warily for a moment before accepting the dark claret. No doubt he was wondering if she'd slipped some sort of poison into his drink. Considering her attitude so far this week, she couldn't blame him.

"What's the occasion?" he asked, taking a small sip.

She leaned back against the overstuffed cushions, balancing her painted toes on the edge of the coffee table, mimicking Connor's relaxed pose.

"Nothing special. I just thought it was awfully nice of you to worry about me when I disappeared into the bathroom for so long, and I wanted to thank you."

"It wouldn't do for my best friend to come home from his honeymoon and discover I'd let his little sister drown," he quipped.

She grinned. "No, I guess it wouldn't. Although, after the way I've treated you since discovering we'd both be staying here for a few days, I'm surprised you didn't come in and try to hold me under."

One side of his mouth quirked up at that. "Thought about it. Didn't want a criminal record."

"Gee, thanks."

Time passed while they enjoyed their wine, the only sound in the room coming from the low volume of the television, playing a family sitcom.

The calm serenity of the moment washed over

her. She hadn't felt this way in far too long...weightless, almost light-headed, without a care in the world. It was a far cry from her life back in L.A., where she had to keep on her toes and almost every waking moment was filled with tension.

She never got to sit and just unwind. Or if she did, it was alone, not in the company of a handsome, average, everyday guy who preferred beer to martinis and pizza to nouveau cuisine. It was comforting to know Connor didn't care what she was wearing, whether her makeup was flawless, or every strand of hair was in place.

As desperately as she'd been avoiding him for nearly a decade, she had to admit she could be herself around him. He'd seen her with scraped knees and gum in her hair. Sobbing her heart out when her pet cat had been killed by a car. While her eyes were red and swollen, her nose running, he'd helped her bury Zoey in the backyard. He'd even seen her throw up macaroni and cheese in the school cafeteria when she was nine, and had been the only student other than her brother not laughing, pointing or making gross gagging noises. Instead, he'd put his arm around her shoulders and walked her to the nurse's office, waiting with her until her mom came to pick her up.

Growing up, he'd been her hero. If she were being honest with herself, she'd have to admit he still was. An imperfect one, true, but still her hero.

Everybody was entitled to a few mistakes in their lifetime, weren't they?

Hmm. Taking another slow sip of wine, she let her head fall back against the couch, balancing the glass on her upper thigh. She must really be feeling relaxed if she was thinking about forgiving him.

But she didn't know if she was ready to be *that* charitable just yet. It was enough that she was even allowing it as an option. She considered that growth—and quite enough growth for one night. After all, Rome wasn't built in a day, and seven-year-old emotional wounds couldn't be healed that quickly, either.

"Do you ever wonder," Connor said in a low murmur, breaking into her thoughts, "what might have happened if we hadn't grown up together? If we'd met each other back then as complete strangers?"

She didn't need him to identify what he meant by "back then." He was talking about that night again.

Surprisingly, her stomach didn't clutch and her temperature didn't begin to rise. Her muscles did tense, but she took another small drink of wine and mentally forced herself to relax.

He obviously needed to talk about it—he'd certainly cornered her often enough—but she had never been in a frame of mind to listen before. She wasn't sure how long she could listen now, either, but at least she was willing to give it a shot.

"I'm not sure I know what you mean," she

said softly, rolling her head on the sofa cushion to look at him.

"I've always thought of you as my sister, Beth. You were Nick's sister by blood, but we grew up together, your family practically adopted me, so it felt like you were my sister, too."

His brandy brown eyes darkened, the corners crinkling slightly as he offered a tight smile. "But we both know I didn't treat you like a sister that night after the football game, in the cab of my truck. I've been wanting to apologize for that for years."

Her heart squeezed for a moment and the old anger and pain tried to break through. She tamped it down, determined not to backslide into her previous attitude and mind-set.

"Why would you apologize? You weren't in the truck by yourself."

"I took advantage of you," he pushed on, glossing over any responsibility she might take for her own actions. "You were young and confused…and a virgin. I was older and more experienced, I should have stopped things before they got out of hand."

With a harsh laugh, she said, "You can get down off the cross now, Connor, no one's blaming you for taking my virginity. I wouldn't have been in your truck if I hadn't wanted to be, and I wouldn't have had sex with you if I hadn't wanted to, either."

From the corner of her eyes, she saw his thumb rubbing absently up and down the stem of his wineglass.

"That still doesn't make it right," he told her. "Your parents have always treated me like one of their own. They trusted me to take care of you, protect you…not to take advantage of you."

"For the last time, you didn't take advantage of me."

With all the negative thoughts she'd had toward him over the years, that had never been one of them.

"Connor," she said in a near whisper, "from the time I turned thirteen, I had a huge crush on you."

It cost her to admit it, but if he'd been living with this guilt for seven years, he deserved to know the truth. Granted, a part of her wanted him to feel guilty, but about other things. About not calling her after their night together. About not making a point of finding out if there were repercussions—such as an unplanned pregnancy—involved.

But this conversation, this delicate peace they seemed to have developed, wasn't about that, it was about setting him straight on what he *was* feeling guilty over.

"I don't know how you could have missed it," she continued with a light laugh. "I was positively cow-eyed over you. I followed you and Nick around like a puppy, wrote 'Mrs. Connor Riordan' in my notebooks a thousand times and did everything I could think of to catch your attention. I *wanted* to be with you that night. If anything, I orchestrated it so that the situation would play out exactly as it did."

He was sitting up on the sofa now, his arms resting on his denim-clad thighs, staring at her. She straightened under his intense gaze, resisting the need to squirm with embarrassment at her admission.

At least he wasn't laughing at her. She wasn't sure she'd have been able to bear that.

But Connor looked anything but amused by her confession. His eyes were blazing, warming her from head to toe with something other than the flush of humiliation.

"I never knew," he said finally, his voice rasping like velvet over sandpaper.

Blowing out a breath, he ran the splayed fingers of one hand through his short, dirty-blond hair. "And I wish to hell I had, because I felt the same damn way."

Shock and disbelief slammed into her like a bolt of lightning. For a moment, she felt dizzy, almost as though she were floating outside of her body.

This wasn't happening, not really. She was still asleep in the tub upstairs, and her dream had segued from memories of the past into some sordid mix of her juvenile hopes and her present circumstances with Connor.

But then he started speaking again, and even though the words roared in her ears, she could hear them, make out what he was saying.

"I watched you grow up and kept telling myself that you were as much as my sister. Your family was my family…I had no business being attracted to you." He paused to take a deep breath. "But I was. God knows I fought it, and I never would have admitted to it, not even under penalty of death, but there it was. Every time you walked down the hall at school or into a classroom. Every time I came over to see your brother and you were bopping around in sweatpants and a skimpy little tank top, I just about swallowed my tongue.

"And then that night after the football game, I couldn't seem to help myself. You were so beautiful, and I'd been wanting you for so long."

All these years, she thought she'd thrown herself at him and he'd only slept with her because…well, he was a man and she'd been available. But the whole time she had a crush on him, he'd been interested in her, too? It was too much to absorb all at once.

She shook her head, trying to clear her mind and her vision. "I can't believe this," she murmured.

He shifted closer to her on the sofa. Their legs touched, the denim of his jeans brushing against her bare skin. He reached out with one hand and covered her thigh just below the hem of her nightie, his thumb drawing circles on the smooth, sensitive flesh of her inner knee.

"I know. All this time we've felt the same way about each other without even realizing it."

He paused for a moment, his gaze zeroing in

on her lips, which suddenly felt so dry, she darted her tongue out to moisten them.

"You know what else?" he asked in a low tone that slid down her spine like warm honey as he leaned in even closer. "I still do…want you."

Seven

As soon as their mouths touched, the years melted away and every fantasy he'd ever had that revolved around Beth flooded his mind.

Her lips were warm beneath his, closed at first, and then parting until their tongues touched. She tasted of the claret they'd been drinking— and something else, something uniquely Beth.

His fingertips slid beneath the hem of her short, sexy nightgown, caressing the silken smoothness of her legs and traveling higher. She seemed as involved in the kiss as he was, her hands cupping the back of his head, tangling in his hair.

With a groan, he pressed her back against the sofa, one arm around her waist to keep her flush with his chest and lower body.

She smelled so good. Fresh from her bath, with her hair still damp in places and falling down her back in a loose, carefree tangle. He could feel the budding of her nipples through the layers of fabric separating their bodies, and he wanted them in his mouth, against his palms.

He abandoned her mouth, only to pay homage to her chin, her jawline, the pouty little lobe of her ear. She arched into him, a purr of pleasure rumbling low in her throat. And then she lifted one leg to hug his hips and the desire already pumping through his veins like a drug shot straight to his groin.

He ground against her, wishing they were naked already so he could be inside her at that very moment. His lips dragged down the column of her neck, the tip of his tongue darting out to trace the line of her collarbone.

From there, he kissed his way to her breast, licking the pearled tip through the slinky material covering her. A wet patch began to grow and he fed it, opening his mouth wider, suckling her until she moaned and held his head in place.

Power surged, lust arcing between them so strongly, he felt almost light-headed. He wanted her—more than he could remember ever wanting another woman. Possibly more than he'd wanted her even back in high school.

Reaching down, he tugged at the bottom of her nightie and dragged the yellow fabric to her waist. His knuckles brushed the sides of her high-cut panties and he started to sweat.

He had to have her. Now, before she changed her mind or he admitted all the reasons they shouldn't be together.

Their hands went for the waistband of his

jeans at the same time. Eyes meeting, chests heaving, they both gave a breathless chuckle.

His pants opened with a snap and her hand was on the zipper covering his straining erection when the doorbell rang.

His heart stuttered to a stop and then sank as her fingers stilled at their task. For a split second, he considered grabbing her up and kissing her silly, until she forgot about the door, forgot about being interrupted, forgot even her own name.

But already the passion was clearing from her gaze, replaced by stark reality. She didn't look horrified, exactly, but she also didn't look ready to roll to the floor and finish what they'd started.

The doorbell buzzed again.

"I think that's the pizza," she said finally, her voice husky with unspent desire.

"Yeah." He held her gaze for another minute, concentrating on his breathing and trying to get some of the blood that had taken up residence south of the border back to his brain.

His chin dropped to his chest when the delivery guy switched from leaning on the bell to pounding on the door frame.

"Coming," he barked, pushing to his feet and crossing the living room. He tugged at the front of his jeans, attempting to alleviate the pressure behind his fly and then dug in his hip pocket for his wallet.

As soon as he opened the door, a gangly teenage boy in a Pizza Palace T-shirt shoved the flat white box at him and snapped out the price. Connor threw in an extra five for the kid's trouble before kicking the door closed with the toe of his boot.

When he turned, Beth was off the couch, arranging her short, shimmery robe to cover the wet spots his mouth had made on her bodice. The memory slugged him in the gut and sent the air from his lungs with a whoosh.

If he had his way, he'd toss the pizza on the kitchen table, stalk back across the living room and sweep her off her feet so they could pick up where they'd left off. He wouldn't give her time to think or breathe or protest.

But Beth didn't look as if she was ready or willing to return to that place of passion where they'd just been.

He sighed. Too bad. He'd thought they were making progress.

"Pizza smells good," he said, hoping to break the tension growing between them. "Wanna get some plates?"

"Sure." The arms that had been hugging her waist fell to her sides as she headed for the kitchen from the opposite direction.

He wasn't offended by her decision to avoid brushing past him. He understood her need for distance, even if he didn't particularly like it.

Crossing back to the sofa, he set the box on the long rectangular coffee table and took a seat to pop open the lid. A second later, Beth sat down beside him, two dinner plates and a stack of napkins in hand.

He served up two slices on each plate, then refilled their wineglasses. Beth accepted the pizza he offered, balancing it on her knees while her eyes remained downcast.

"Maybe I should take mine up to my room," she murmured, brushing a lock of hair behind one ear. "You could finish watching your television show or whatever."

She wouldn't look at him, and Connor nearly cursed.

Where had the hot, frantic woman from only moments ago gone? Or even the prickly, sharp-tongued one from earlier in the day?

"No, don't do that," he said, brushing his hand down the length of her arm. His touch didn't linger, and he was relieved that she didn't stiffen up on him. "Stay here. We'll stick in a DVD and stuff ourselves silly."

At first, she didn't answer him. Then she raised her head, met his eyes and curled her lips in a small smile. "All right. But I get to pick the film."

He threw himself against the back of the couch, clutching his chest and giving an exaggerated groan. "Oh, no. Not some girlie movie."

Her grin widened. "Maybe."

She took a bite off the tip of her pizza slice, then got up and sauntered to the entertainment center on the other side of the room.

Connor watched her go, admiring the sway of her bottom and the long, pale line of her legs. She looked like a million bucks, and in that sunny-colored nightgown, good enough to eat. Next to her, the pizza he'd been so hungry for only an hour before might as well have been cardboard.

After shuffling around in the cupboard, she placed a disc in the player on top of the television, then made her way back to the sofa. She kept her distance this time, leaving one full cushion between them before retrieving her glass of wine and pressing Play on the remote control.

"Should I be worried?" he asked around a

mouthful of cheese and crust and assorted toppings.

Her shoulder lifted and fell, but her eyes never left the television screen. "Depends."

The opening credits began to play, along with music he recognized. He grinned as he realized she'd chosen one of his favorites…Keanu Reeves and Sandra Bullock trying to stay alive on a speeding bus. It was an action/adventure flick, but could probably also be categorized as a romance.

"A woman after my own heart," he told her, taking an even bigger bite of pizza.

"I'm a Curtis," she retorted, "so of course I have exceptional taste."

"Uh-huh. I'm just glad I didn't let you order the pizza. We might have ended up with some horrible tofu-and-pineapple concoction."

"Don't scoff. Tofu is good for you."

"I'll stick with my meat and vegetables, thanks."

"Suit yourself." She picked at a green pepper melted into the cheese of what was left of her first slice. "You know, I'm going to have to run ten miles tomorrow to burn this off."

Even as she said it, she lifted the crust to her lips, so he knew she must not be too concerned.

"Maybe I'll go with you." He blurted it out before he had a chance to rethink the idea, but when she shot him a look of pure disbelief, he almost wished he'd kept his mouth shut.

So he didn't make a habit of jogging. He worked hard on a daily basis, building and renovating houses—carrying lumber, shingles, climbing ladders... And he stopped at the gym once in a while, though probably not as often as he should. No, he didn't tend to put on shorts and sneakers and go running around the neighborhood—but for Beth, he'd be willing to give it a try.

"What?" he asked, feigning insult. "You don't think I can run?"

"Oh, I'm sure you can run. Away from a bear. Toward a cold beer. But for exercise?" She laughed, and then covered her mouth with a napkin when she started to choke. "No, I'm sorry, I can't picture that."

He quirked a brow, staring hard until her gaze faltered. "Fine. I'll just have to prove it to you. What time do you want to go in the morning?"

"Six."

That wasn't even particularly early for him. He was up before that lots of mornings in order to get to job sites on time.

"Six it is."

She eyed him warily over the rim of her wineglass. "You're really going through with this, huh?"

"Just see if you can keep up."

Beth was trying hard not to laugh. She concentrated on her pace and her breathing, struggling not to burst a lung with the effort to hide her amusement.

He was hanging in there, she'd give him that.

He'd been up bright and early this morning,

already dressed in shorts and a T-shirt when she'd come downstairs. The sneakers were Nick's, found in a hall closet, he told her, but they seemed to fit well enough. Connor and Nick had always been about the same size, sharing clothes and shoes and everything else.

They'd grabbed bottles of water before heading out, then started at a slow trot from the curb. It was still dusky outside, with just a hint of sunrise peeking through on the bluish purple horizon.

And it was chilly. That odd time of year when true winter has passed, but spring hadn't quite made its birds-and-flowers appearance yet. The ground was wet, the air chilly, the sky studded with clouds.

At first, Connor did great. He even seemed to be doing better than she was, since she was used to running on a state-of-the-art treadmill at the gym with her headset to keep her company instead of an unswept, leaf- and gravel-strewn sidewalk with the sounds of dogs barking and car doors slamming as neighbors left for work.

Jogging side by side, they chatted about the weather—typical for central Ohio at this time of year, but a far cry from the sunny California she was used to—and some of the items they needed to pick up at the hardware store later that day to start work on the nursery.

Then she'd kicked it up a notch, increasing her pace and working her arms for the added burn. She gave him credit for his effort, but it wasn't long before he fell behind and started heaving for breath.

Not that he was out of shape. Far from it, judging by his firm thighs and calves, and the rippling muscles outlined beneath his sweat-dampened T-shirt. He was simply used to a different kind of exercise—hauling and sawing and hammering.

She pictured him in his usual uniform of faded jeans and open flannel shirt, doing what he did best amidst sawhorses and power tools, and nearly lost her footing.

Righting herself, she glanced at Connor from her peripheral vision and decided he'd had enough. They'd been out for at least an hour, and stubborn as he was, he would probably keep running until it killed him, just to prove a point.

She slowed a bit, waiting for him to catch up as the house came into view. It was lighter now, though still overcast, with a hint of rain in the air. Likely that storm the lady at the airline had warned her about…though she still thought she should have been able to get a flight out before it hit.

"You doing okay?" she asked, knowing full well what his answer would be.

"Oh, yeah," he huffed, beads of sweat rolling down his face. "I could keep running like this all day."

Sure he could. She turned her head so he wouldn't see her grin.

"That's great," she said, "but I think we've

had enough for today. With any luck, we've burned off at least one slice of pizza and one glass of wine from last night."

They stopped at the walk to her brother's house. She continued to jog in place until her heart rate slowed while Connor bent at the waist, hands on his knees as he fought to fill his lungs with oxygen.

Her breathing was labored, too, but she was used to it. She loved it, actually, found it exhilarating.

"I say we get cleaned up and go into town."

Part of the reason she'd wanted to go running was to offset some of her anxiety about not only spending the day shopping and working with Connor, but about buying baby things and concentrating on designing a nursery.

She knew it would be difficult, was already bracing herself for the pain. Surprisingly, though, she now felt more prepared for the task. Not exactly looking forward to it, but stronger and better able to handle whatever emotions the day stirred up.

"Sounds good. Do you want first dibs on the shower?"

He straightened, wiping his forehead with the tail of his shirt, giving her a clear glimpse of those tight, well-defined abdominals she'd fantasized about earlier. It was enough to make a girl drool.

She took a long swig of water to wet her parched throat, wiping the corners of her mouth afterward, just in case.

"No, you go ahead."

He looked as if he needed it more. And besides, she could use a few minutes alone before getting undressed and stepping into the shower. If she went upstairs now, she would have to turn the spray to full cold, but if she waited a while, she might be able to go with moderate to lukewarm.

"You sure?"

She nodded, starting up the front steps and fitting the key in the lock.

Brushing past her, he made his way through the house and up the stairs. She listened to his footfalls, followed by the sound of the water coming on in the bathroom.

While he was busy in the shower, she put their half-empty bottles of water in the fridge, then went to her room to lay out an outfit for the rest of the day. She hadn't packed work clothes… wasn't sure she even owned true down-and-dirty work clothes anymore. But she found a pair of navy blue slacks and a lightweight tan knit top that would hopefully be casual enough—as long as Connor didn't put her to work painting or scrubbing.

The water in the bathroom cut off, and she heard him moving around for a few minutes before the door opened. When she glanced up, he was standing in the hall just outside her bedroom.

His close-cropped hair was wet, making it appear more dark brown than dirty blond. A drop of water fell from one of the spiky locks, rolling down his temple, cheek and stubbled jawline before dripping onto his bare chest.

What a fine chest it was, too. Broad and firm. Smooth in places, a sprinkling of light hair in others.

She watched the drop of water slide past one flat, bronze nipple to the plane of his washboard stomach. A few inches below, a stark white towel was wrapped around his hips.

"The bathroom is all yours," he said in a low tone.

Licking her lips, she dragged her gaze back to his face. His eyes smoldered, lips twisted in the hint of a grin.

Great. Not only had she ogled him, but he'd caught her at it.

Way to maintain your distance, Beth, she thought with derision.

Then again, their little makeout session on the couch last night hadn't exactly screamed *disinterest.*

"Thanks," she said, embarrassed when her voice actually squeaked.

She'd moved to L.A. to get away from Connor and had matured by leaps and bounds. But ever since returning to Crystal Springs, she seemed to be regressing to her pathetic, high-school-crush persona.

All the more reason to get out of here and fly back to California as soon as possible. Maybe then she could regain a bit of her equilibrium.

Seconds ticked by while they stood there staring at each other. They didn't speak, didn't move until stars started to burst behind Beth's eyeballs and she realized she'd been holding her breath almost the entire time.

With conscious effort, she exhaled and began to breathe normally. Turning, she gathered the pile of fresh clothes from the bed, then slipped through the doorway and toward the bathroom, careful not to touch Connor's bare arm or chest as she passed.

"I'll only be a few minutes," she told him.

"Take your time."

She cast one last glance over her shoulder before closing the bathroom door, and a shiver raced down her spine at the look of lustful intent on his face.

Worse yet was the echo of that expression strumming low in her belly.

The door clicked shut, and she released a weary sigh.

It looked as if she'd be taking that cold shower, after all.

"Clowns are passé."

"Oh, and teddy bears are all the rage?"

Beth cocked a hip and crossed her arms beneath her breasts. "At least they're cute and cuddly." She pointed to one of the clowns on the border wallpaper he was holding. "Those are downright scary."

He lowered his gaze and studied the colorful artwork for a minute, then stuck the roll back on the rack. "You're right. These clowns would probably give the kid nightmares. But I can't say I love the bears."

The teddy-bear border in her hand was cute—soft and cuddly in an array of pastels. But he had a point; they were kind of boring and probably like every other border in every other nursery in the world.

"All right. No clowns and no teddy bears. What are our other options?"

They started to investigate their choices again, and she thought—not for the first time—how much she was enjoying herself.

She hadn't expected to. If anything, she'd been prepared for the day to be akin to shoving bamboo shoots under her fingernails.

After they were both cleaned up, dressed and had grabbed a quick breakfast of toast and orange juice, they'd headed for the hardware store. Beth pretty much let Connor take the lead there, since he made his living building things.

Her knowledge of carpentry didn't extend much beyond the difference between a hammer and measuring tape.

He'd bought supplies to make some new shelving, and to pull up the old carpet and refinish the hardwood floor beneath. If the floor was in too much disrepair to be left bare, he'd told her, they'd go out and buy new carpeting later.

But now they were in Crystal Springs's one and only retail store, and she'd taken over the shopping list. They were holding off buying furniture…partly because there wouldn't be space to store it until the room was finished, and partly because she didn't think they could be completely sure what type of crib, changing table or rocking chair they needed until everything else was done. They were waiting to decide on curtains and area rugs for the same reason.

Unfortunately, they'd made the mistake of buying paint already at the hardware store. In retrospect, they'd have been better off waiting until they picked out a border or other items before settling on a color for the room. It was too late now, though; the soft seafoam, a cross between green and blue that would be perfect for either a boy or a girl, was already mixed and waiting in the back of Connor's truck.

"What about this?" Beth asked, holding up a roll of paper for him to see, along with the paint sample they'd brought along from the hardware store. "The blues and greens will match," she said. "And the little sea creatures are just adorable."

There were playful dolphins and turtles, orcas and jellyfish…even a few sharks and octopi that anyone would find charming.

Connor met her gaze and gave her one of those sexy, lopsided grins that filled her belly with butterfly wings. "I like it. We could even buy a bunch of stuffed animals for the crib and shelves and rocker to match."

"You don't think Nick and Karen will be upset that we're choosing the theme of the nursery for them?" she asked, voicing a concern she'd had since the beginning.

"Nah. They'll love it. And if there's anything they don't like, we just have to make it clear that we won't be hurt or offended if they change it. After all, it is their house and their baby."

"Yeah," she agreed, fighting not to let the moment turn bittersweet. "We should probably keep that in mind."

"We will. Now grab up a bunch of those so we can get moving."

She did as he requested, filling her arms with the number of wallpaper rolls they'd agreed earlier should do the trick and dumping them in the shopping cart.

"Only one thing left on the list." He stood with legs splayed, hands on hips, studying her from head to toe.

"What?" She looked down at herself. Had she spilled orange juice on her sweater earlier?

"Are those the best work clothes you have,

or were you going to change when we get back home?"

Biting her bottom lip, she linked her arms self-consciously across her waist. "I'm afraid this is it. I didn't exactly pack for my brother's wedding with the intention of getting sweaty and dirty." And she didn't exactly spend a lot of time getting sweaty and dirty back in L.A., unless it was at her personal trainer's command.

Connor's nostrils flared at that, his eyes wandering back to the area of her breasts. She bit her lip to keep from fidgeting under his concentrated scrutiny.

"Well, that won't do. Sorry. We're going to have to buy you some jeans and T-shirts."

"Are you sure?" She cast another glance at her dark slacks with their nearly razor-sharp creases down the front from where they'd been pressed and folded with almost military precision, and the expensive sweater she really wasn't looking forward to ruining.

"Yep. It's gotta be done." Pressing his palm to the mesh end of the cart, he gave it a little shove, nudging her in the side. "Come on…to women's clothing we go."

She turned obediently and started walking in the direction he pointed.

"Do you really want to take the time for me to try on work clothes?" she asked, half hoping he'd change his mind.

Instead, he speared her with a cocky grin, keeping the cart on course. "Oh, yeah. I'm looking forward to it. If I'm lucky, I figure you might even let me in the dressing room with you to see how everything fits."

She shot him a quelling glare. "Keep dreaming, bub."

But as she slipped between the racks of blue jeans to hunt for a pair in her size, she thought she heard him murmur, "Oh, I will, believe me."

Eight

The sounds of sawing and hammering echoed through the house, along with music from a radio they'd set up in the hall. They'd been working for three days straight, and Beth had to admit the room was looking good.

Connor was in charge, no doubt about it. But he was a good boss, explaining what needed to be done and showing her how to handle certain things without growing short on patience or making her feel stupid.

So far, they'd taken down the plain, dusty white curtains from the windows, pulled up the old, worn carpet from the floor and repolished the golden wood beneath. Now the floor was covered with plastic and drop cloths, and Connor had set up sawhorses and a wide array of tools to use while he worked.

At the moment, he was standing on a ladder on the far side of the room, looking sexier than any man had a right to. His gray cotton shirt molded to his back and biceps like a second skin, and his jeans rode low on his narrow hips, showcasing his truly spectacular rear. And if that wasn't enough to drive every sensible thought from her mind, the tool belt strapped around his waist actually turned her on. She could watch him remove and replace tools from the worn leather all day.

There was just something about a man who was good with his hands…

Shaking her head, she turned back to what she was supposed to be doing. Connor was tacking up beautiful crown molding and she was putting the first coat of seafoam paint on the walls. The artfully carved strips of wood he was handling were bare now, but later they would paint them white to create a bright, clean border along the ceiling.

She dipped her roller in the pan of paint on the floor and took up where she'd left off before Connor's fluid, masculine movements had distracted her.

He'd been right about her needing a set of work clothes, too. As careful as she tried to be, after three days of manual labor, she was covered with specks of paint, streaks of dirt and a layer of sawdust. She'd even managed to snag her bright red Hot Stuff ballerina tee in two different places.

As she transformed the walls from boring eggshell to a green-blue sea fit for the marine life they would eventually add, she hummed along and danced a little to the B-52's song playing in the background.

"You having fun over here?"

Connor's voice, coming from just over her left shoulder, caused her to jump and splash more paint on herself.

"Geez," she yelped, pressing her free hand to her heart. "You scared the life out of me."

"Sorry," he said with a sneaky grin that told her he wasn't sorry at all. His gaze moved back to the wall she'd been working on. "Looks good. You should come to work for Nick and me."

"Thanks."

She grinned with obvious pleasure, the light in her eyes slipping under his skin and twisting his guts.

God, she was beautiful. Over the last seven years, he thought he'd made more of her appearance than there was. Imagined the glossy russet of her hair, the periwinkle blue of her eyes, the sparkle in her smile.

But if anything, she looked better than he remembered. Confident, alluring…she'd really grown into herself.

When he'd finished with the last piece of molding and turned to see how she was doing with the walls, he'd just about fallen off the ladder. She was stroking the paint roller up and down, and doing some kind of little jiggle in time with the music from the radio that had her hips swaying and her bottom rocking, the hem of her top riding up to show an inch of creamy torso.

It was enough to send him into cardiac arrest, which was why he'd slipped his hammer into his tool belt and very carefully climbed down off the ladder before he tripped over his wagging tongue and broke his neck.

He cleared his throat, dragging his attention back to the present. "If you're about finished, I say we wrap things up for today and start getting ready to head over to the Longneck. You're still meeting your friends there, right?"

She looked startled for the space of a heartbeat before lowering the paint roller and sticking her hands in the back pockets of those low-riding jeans.

"Oh, yeah. I didn't realize it was so late already. What time is it?"

With a quick glance at his watch, he said, "Almost six. We probably have time to grab a quick bite after we get cleaned up and dressed, unless you plan to order dinner at the bar."

"We probably will get something to eat there. You're welcome to join us," she added in a low voice.

At first he thought she was only being polite, but he could tell by the look in her eyes that the offer was sincere. And for a minute, he seriously considered taking her up on it, if only as an excuse to stay close to her.

"Thanks, but I think I'll pass," he finally forced himself to respond. "You and your friends probably want a little time alone to bash men and discuss panty lines."

She laughed, wiping the back of her wrist across her nose. The gesture left a small streak of seafoam paint behind.

"Is that what you really think women talk about when they get together?"

He shrugged. "I'm close, aren't I?" he murmured, distracted by that tiny smudge and the energy it took to keep from reaching out and wiping it away.

"Only if one of us has recently been dumped. Then, I admit, we're none too charitable about the opposite sex. But other than that, we don't usually spend much time disparaging the male race."

"So what do you talk about?"

"Our jobs, our families. Once in a while we do discuss the latest fashions, but that's usually after we've had a couple of drinks or run out of other topics of conversation."

"Good to know," he said, and then gave in to temptation by lifting a hand and brushing the paint from the tip of her nose. When she gave him an odd look, he held up his fingers to show the blue-green tint.

"Thanks." She rubbed absently at the spot herself. "Guess we both need a shower."

Connor's blood thickened and pooled low in his belly at her words. Being this close to her, watching her breasts rise and fall as she breathed, smelling her spicy floral perfume was sheer torture.

He wanted to do more than reach out and swipe paint from her nose. He wanted to grab her up and kiss her senseless. Run his fingers through that long, silky mass of chestnut hair. Suggest they conserve water and shower together…or skip bathing altogether and head straight for the bedroom.

Swallowing hard, he made himself stop that train of thought before it got out of hand. Or worse, he acted on it.

That night on the couch had been a fluke.

They'd had wine on empty stomachs and gotten a little carried away.

For God's sake, Beth had barely spoken to him during the last seven years, and he was living with another woman. At least, he had been until very recently.

This…whatever it was…must be residual attraction from their teenage and young-adult years. Unresolved issues from their one night together.

As soon as she flew back to California—which would probably be sooner rather than later—whatever was between them would pass. The electricity, the longing, the teeth-rattling, knee-buckling lust.

They would both get over it and go on with their respective lives, so it was better not to start anything now, no matter how much he might wish it could be otherwise. Especially something that would cause them to avoid each other for another seven to ten years.

The same as in high school, he never wanted

to do anything to hurt her or her family. Nothing to cause tension or pain between them… between any of them. Beth and him, Nick and him, Beth and her parents, or her parents and him.

It was a tangled, convoluted mess, and he felt like a fly struggling uselessly to free itself from the sticky web of a hungry spider. Except that he was as responsible for spinning this particular web as anyone else.

Unfastening his tool belt, he lowered it carefully to the newly polished hardwood floor. "We should probably start getting ready," he told her, though it was the last thing he wanted to do.

He would much prefer to spend the evening just like this. With Beth, standing close, looking into her eyes, maybe curling up on the couch to watch another movie. Even if nothing happened between them—which it wouldn't, *couldn't*—being alone with Beth still beat hanging out at the Longneck any day of the week.

"Right."

She glanced away guiltily and turned to clean up her work area, but not before he saw the tip of her tongue dart out to wet her lips.

Damn. He had to get out of here before he did something stupid, like pulling her up from where she now crouched on the floor, pressing her back against the wall, and taking her the way he'd imagined for over a decade.

Man, he was warped. He'd just finished convincing himself he needed to walk away, keep his distance, yet here he was picturing her with her top yanked up and her legs wrapped around his waist.

Struggling for breath, he asked, "Do you need any help?"

She cocked her head, fixing him with those soft blue eyes. "No, that's all right. Thanks, though. I just want to get the lid on this paint, then I'll stick the roller and brushes in the sink to soak while I get cleaned up. How about you?"

"I'm good." Or doomed. He hitched a thumb over his right shoulder. "I'll start getting ready. It shouldn't take me more than a few minutes, then I can be out of your way."

Beth nodded. "Take your time. Gail and Jackie won't care if I'm a little late."

Inclining his head, he turned and started through the doorway to the hall.

"Oh, and Connor?" she called after him.

He turned back, giving her his undivided attention. "Yeah?"

"Women don't usually talk about panty lines when they get together because we already know how to avoid them."

"How's that?" he asked, his voice thick with restrained arousal.

"Simple. Don't wear panties."

She shot him a quick, wicked smile, then turned back to what she was doing while he stood there like a deer caught in headlights.

Damn.

* * *

The Longneck was already jumping when they walked in a few minutes after eight. Music blared from the jukebox along the far wall, couples two-stepped across the dance floor, and just about every table and seat at the bar was occupied.

"Wow, it's really busy for a Wednesday night." She leaned close to Connor, raising her voice to be heard over the din of the music and crowd. His arm was at her waist, but she let it go, telling herself it was a protective gesture only, to keep her from getting jostled around by the bar's exuberant patrons.

"You should see it on Friday and Saturday nights. This is tame in comparison."

She returned his grin with one of her own. She'd forgotten what it meant to go out and have fun in Crystal Springs. No stiletto heels, skin-tight sheaths or sparkling diamonds necessary. No fancy mixed drinks in even fancier glasses. In central Ohio, jeans were dressy enough for both men and women, and beer was the beverage of choice, whether it came in a bottle or a frosted glass.

This type of thing hadn't been her scene for a very long time, so she was surprised by how comfortable she felt the minute she walked through the door. Even the loud country music, which normally would have set her on the fast track to a migraine, seemed to seep into her bones instead. She found herself tapping her toe already.

"Are your friends here yet?" he wanted to know.

"One of them is." She pointed across the room at the booth her friend had staked out for them. From the looks of it, Jackie had gotten the ball rolling on their girls' night out with a bottle of light beer and a tray of nachos.

With a slight pressure at the small of her back, Connor accompanied her through the crowd.

"Beth!" As soon as Jackie spotted her, she jumped up and threw her arms around her friend. "It's so good to see you again. I missed you so much!"

Beth laughed with genuine happiness. "I missed you, too. You look great."

"Me?" Jackie glanced down at herself, brushing her hands over the hem of her sweater where it hugged her well-rounded hips. "Honey, I've had four kids…I haven't looked great since high school."

It was obvious her friend was joking and was actually quite comfortable with her robust figure, so Beth felt safe chuckling in response. But she couldn't resist adding a gentle chastise-ment. "Don't say that. You're still beautiful, your children are adorable, and your husband is hopelessly devoted. You're one of the luckiest women in this town, and you darn well know it."

Jackie's cheeks turned crimson and the corners of her mouth lifted in a goofy grin. "Yeah, I know it. But you…" She stood back, eyeing Beth from head to toe. "L.A. agrees with you. You look like one of those gorgeous runway models, putting everyone here to shame."

Since the only pair of jeans she currently owned was spattered with paint, Beth had opted for a tailored gray pantsuit with a pale blue blouse to add a touch of color, and her black, all-purpose sling-backs. She felt slightly out of place among the sweatshirts and western wear, but not nearly as much as she'd expected. Here, she was simply one of the girls, a Crystal Springs native, no matter how she was dressed.

"Thanks. Jackie, you know Connor Riordan, don't you?" she asked, pulling Connor forward a few steps in hopes of diverting her friend's attention.

"Of course." She reached out to take the hand he offered. "How are you, Connor?"

"Just fine, thanks. And you?"

They chatted for a few brief minutes before Beth spotted Gail at the entrance of the restaurant. She lifted an arm and waved until her friend saw them and started in their direction.

Again, Beth made the introductions, and then Gail and Jackie slipped into the booth and waved for a waitress to bring them more drinks.

"I'll call you when I need a ride home," Beth told Connor. "Or get one of the girls to drop me off."

"No, that's all right," he said. "I think I'll stick around a while. Have a drink, catch up with old friends. I'll let you know when I'm ready to leave, and you can either come with me or make other arrangements."

She nodded, watching him cross the room toward the bar and feeling oddly bereft at the loss of his hand at her waist. Shaking off the bizarre emotion, she pasted a smile on her face and slipped onto the padded bench seat next to her friend.

She'd been looking forward to this evening all week, and would be darned if she'd let her mixed-up, indecisive feelings about Connor ruin it for her.

* * *

After laughing and joking and catching up on any number of things that had happened since the last time they saw each other, Jackie and Gail both said they had to get home.

Beth was immediately disappointed. She didn't want to leave; she was having too good a time. Even given the nachos and beer instead of the cosmopolitans and finger sandwiches she was used to, hanging out at the Longneck was just plain *fun*.

She hugged her friends and walked them to the door to say goodbye. It was raining out, she noticed as Jackie and Gail darted across the parking lot, holding their jackets over their heads to keep from getting drenched. Then she turned back around and scanned the still-crowded room for Connor.

He said he'd let her know before he took off, and since she hadn't seen him since then, she assumed he was still here. Maybe at the bar, or on the dance floor, or in one of the back rooms playing pool.

If the Longneck even still had pool tables. Good Lord, she hadn't been home or to her old haunts in so long, she couldn't be sure what changes had been made. For all she knew, the pool tables that had been so popular when she was in college had been replaced by video or pinball games.

Returning to the table she'd shared with the girls, she grabbed up her half-full bottle of light beer, making her way toward the back rooms. She scanned the crowd as she walked, looking for Connor's short, dirty-blond hair and blue chambray shirt as she passed.

He wasn't at the bar or any of the tables, and she didn't see him on the dance floor. Good thing. She wasn't sure she could handle the sight of him with his arms around another woman.

What a silly notion, she thought, pausing long enough to scan the sea of people and take another sip of beer. She had no claim on him. Didn't want to lay claim to him. If anything, it would be best for them to each go their separate ways.

But even though she'd been telling herself for years that she was over him, she still didn't like the idea of seeing some other woman curled around him like a weed.

It had been that way back in high school, too. Connor hadn't seemed to notice she was alive, but it ate her up inside any time he'd come around with a new girlfriend. Some tall, skinny, blond cheerleader who giggled like an idiot and never sat down unless she could be draped across his lap.

Beth stopped at the wide-open entryway to the dance area, which also led off to back rooms on either side. A slow country ballad was playing, and couples swayed together to the languid beat.

When she didn't spot Connor among the dancers, she headed left, toward the pool room. And it was still a pool room, she noticed with nostalgic pleasure. Six or eight men stood around watching four others play through at two different tables. Biker leather and silver studs mixed with cowboy boots and hats.

Connor was leaning over the edge of one of the tables, lining up his shot. He struck out and the ball he'd been aiming for sailed straight into a corner pocket. Half the audience in the room groaned while the other half high-fived.

Connor grinned, retrieving his beer from the side of the table and taking a celebratory swig. He turned to lean against the wall while his opponent took his shot, and spotted her.

"Hey," he said, pushing away and crossing the space of the room to her side. "You and your friends ready to head home?"

She nodded. "Gail and Jackie already left."

He glanced over his shoulder. It was his turn at the table again, but he looked back at her first. "Do you want to leave? I can get someone else to cover the rest of the game for me."

For a moment, she considered his offer. "How much do you have riding on it?"

A slight flush reddened his cheekbones, and then his mouth lifted up in a grin. "Fifty bucks."

"Go ahead and finish," she told him with a smile of her own, tipping the brown bottle she was holding in his direction. "Win some money and maybe you can buy me another drink."

"How many have you had so far?" he wanted to know.

"Only two or three."

"You coming or not?" the bearded man he had the bet going with called out.

"Yeah," Connor retorted. "Just a minute." Turning his attention back to Beth, he said, "All right. As soon as I finish this game, I'll buy you another drink...on one condition."

"What's that?"

"You dance with me first."

She glanced over her shoulder at the dance floor, taking in all the couples moving in tandem to a style of music that was quickly growing on her. It was probably a mistake to agree, considering her recent train of thought, but she couldn't seem to help herself. She'd never gotten to dance with him all those years ago, and even though it was too late for everything, in every sense of the word, she still wanted what those girls in high school had experienced.

Just one dance. What could it hurt?

Meeting his soft brown gaze, she inclined her head. "Deal."

He flashed her a wide, pearly-white smile. "Back in a minute. This shouldn't take long."

True to his word, the game ended in another ten minutes, with Connor winning and collecting fifty dollars from his defeated but good-natured opponent. He passed his stick off to the next guy in line for a round at the tables and made his way over to Beth.

"Congratulations," she said, watching him add the bills to his wallet.

"Told you it wouldn't take long. Ready for that dance?"

Her chest tightened at his intense expression and a skittering of anxiousness skated along her nerve endings. The current song on the jukebox was coming to an end, putting her even more on the spot. Not that she was actually considering backing out.

Bending her knees, she crouched down just far enough to set her empty beer bottle on the floor beside the open archway to the pool room. Hopefully a waitress would be by to gather them, but if not, they should be out of the way enough not to trip anyone up before closing.

Connor did the same before taking her hand and starting toward the jukebox. There was one song left before new selections would begin to play.

"The next song is a fast one, but I had something slow in mind for our dance," he said, feeding quarters into the machine and punching the button for his choice. "What do you say? Would you be willing to dance with me twice in a row?"

What the heck. Maybe dancing to a fast song, away from him and without touching, would prepare her for the moment when his arms would go around her and their bodies would press together.

"Sure," she answered with more conviction than she felt.

The upward tilt of his lips in response made her stomach flutter, and she drew a deep breath to keep her lungs functioning properly. He wrapped his fingers around her elbow and led her to the center of the dance floor.

He slid his hand from her elbow, down the length of her arm, and over her wrist, raising shivers and gooseflesh everywhere he touched. Linking his fingers with hers, he gave a small tug, causing her to stumble into the solid wall of his chest.

So much for keeping her distance through the

first song. Instead of standing by themselves, dancing independently as she'd expected, he kept her hand grasped in his own and curled the other over the curve of her hip as they bounced and jiggled.

If this was how he danced with a woman to a quick, upbeat tune, she could only imagine where his hands would be during a more subdued ballad. And since she'd promised him a slow song, she supposed she'd soon find out.

"So did you have a good time with your friends?" he spoke against her ear.

It wasn't easy to carry on a conversation this close to the source of the loud music, but she nodded. "It was good to catch up with them."

A minute later, the song came to an end and there was a brief pause while the next set up. Connor didn't loosen his hold, and when the slow song began, he pulled her even closer.

"Ah, here we go. This is what I've been waiting for."

He slid the hand at her hip around to her back until his arm completely encircled her waist. The position brought them together like playing cards, her breasts pressed flat, their lower bodies brushing in a sensual, intimate way.

She tried at first to pull away, to put just a modicum of distance between them, but he wouldn't let her go. And then, as the music filled the room and began to seep into her soul, she gave up. Surrendered.

It was only a dance. One she'd agreed to and been looking forward to, at that.

It was also Connor…her brother's best friend, one of *her* best friends through most of her childhood, and one of the people she used to trust most in the world. If she wasn't safe in his arms, she wasn't safe in anyone's.

Nine

He knew the exact moment the tension drained from Beth's body and she began to relax. Her spine—which she'd been holding almost ramrod straight—bent slightly beneath his palm. The muscles in her arms became less rigid, and she settled against him instead of trying so hard to hold herself away.

He wanted to whoop with triumph, sigh with relief. But to avoid spooking her back into skittish-colt mode, he merely continued to dance, enjoying her closeness.

She smelled of that same spicy floral scent he was coming to associate with her, even after hours of hanging out in a smoky bar. Her hair fell around her face and over her shoulders in wavy mahogany curls, perfectly framing her robin's-egg eyes and flawless, heart-shaped face.

They swayed together to the music, letting the slow beat and soulful voice of the singer direct their movements. The thumb of his left hand stroked slowly up and down, caressing her back.

He wished she weren't wearing the jacket that went with her suit so he could feel her skin more easily through the tissue-paper thinness of her blouse. Better yet, she should be nude...they should both be nude so he could feel her petal-soft skin beneath his hands, her pert breasts pressing into his bare chest.

She lifted her head and their gazes met. If he hadn't already been painfully aroused from his fantasies about having her naked in his arms while they danced, then the look in her eyes would have done it. They were warm and tender and vulnerable.

Maybe it was the beer she'd been drinking with her friends, or maybe she was starting to remember what it was like to live in a small town, to be around people you knew and who cared about you. She might even be remembering what things had been like between the two of them before it went so wrong.

The chords of the song strummed to an end and everyone stopped dancing, returning to their tables or waiting for the next song to begin. Beth and Connor had already slowed and now stood still, staring at each other.

Clearing his throat, he said, "Song's over. Wanna dance again?"

She shook her head.

"Want a drink?"

She shook her head again.

"Want to go home?"

She nodded and the gesture sent a jolt of excitement rocking through his system.

He didn't want to assume anything…didn't want to take for granted that just because she was asking him to take her home, she also meant to go to bed with him. Though it *was* numbers one through ten on his wish list at the moment, for all he knew, she wanted to go back to the house to sleep off whatever alcohol she'd consumed this evening.

But he also wasn't going to look a gift horse in the mouth. She might not be suggesting they make love, but it had been a hell of a night already, in his estimation, and he would rather leave now than stick around and risk something happening to tarnish the memory of it.

"Okay," he murmured, still standing in the middle of the dance floor, still gazing down at her face, still holding her tight. "Let's get out of here."

Keeping a grip on her hand, he turned and headed through the crowd, toward the main entrance at the other end of the bar. Beth stayed close on his heels, bumping into him when he stepped back to open the door. A gust of cold air blew in, along with a good amount of the rain that was pouring down in buckets outside.

"Whoa."

"Oh, I forgot. It's raining," she said, as though he couldn't see that for himself. He was getting damp just standing inside the open door.

"No kidding." He glanced at her over his shoulder. "Did you bring a coat?"

"No. I didn't think I'd need one."

Neither had he. It had been cool when they'd left the house, but he hadn't expected to be out this late. He also hadn't expected this much of a deluge.

"Stay here," he told her. "I'll get the truck and bring it around." At least that way she would stay mostly dry.

But she shook her head, sending the long locks of her hair bouncing. "I'm not a sugar cube, I won't melt."

It was a saying he'd heard her father utter a million times…but to his recollection, Beth had always balked at getting too wet and wouldn't go out without a hat or umbrella.

"You sure?" he asked her.

"Yep. Let's get out of here before we flood the place."

He smiled, squeezed her hand and took off at a run across the parking lot. They both held their free hands over their heads to ward off as much of the downpour as possible, but it was a wasted effort. The rain soaked through their clothes and wet their skin long before they reached the truck.

Unlocking the passenger-side door, he helped her into the cab, then ran around the front of the vehicle and jumped behind the wheel.

"Whoo!" He shook himself like a dog after a bath, sending droplets of water spraying everywhere. "Guess this is the storm those meteorologists have been talking about all week."

She chuckled, wiping her face and wringing moisture out of her own hair. When he noticed her rubbing her arms to ward off a chill, he started the engine and turned the heat on high.

They drove home in near silence, wipers working furiously to keep the windshield clear. When they reached the house, he pulled into the driveway and parked as close to the front door as possible.

The neighborhood was dark, but he didn't know if that was due to the late hour, or a possible storm-induced power outage. He also couldn't remember if he'd turned on the porch light before leaving. It was off now, though.

"Ready for this?" he asked after shutting off the engine and separating the house key from the rest.

"I can't get any wetter than I already am," she replied.

And then they were out of the truck and jogging for the porch. He got the front door open, stepping aside for her to precede him.

The warmth of the house enveloped them, a welcome change from the cold of the driving rain. They stood in the entryway for a moment, laughing and dripping.

Connor reached over to flip the switch for the kitchen lights, but nothing happened. He flipped it again for good measure, then tried the others on the same panel.

"Looks like the electricity is out."

"I'm not surprised. That wind is enough to knock over entire power stations."

Shrugging out of her soggy jacket, she tiptoed across the linoleum kitchen floor, dropping it into the sink. Lifting one leg and then the other, she peeled off her black high heels and left them dangling by the straps from her fingertips.

"I'll run upstairs to change and get some towels," she said. "Do you want me to bring anything down for you?"

"No, thanks," he said. "I'll run up and change myself soon, but first I think I'd better get a fire started in the fireplace. With the power out, the furnace won't be running, and even though it's warm enough in here now, if this storm rages all night, it's bound to get chilly."

"Sounds great."

"Do you need a flashlight?" he asked. His eyes had acclimated enough to the inky blackness that he could see the quick smile she tossed his way.

"Are you kidding? Nick and I used to sneak around the house in the dark all the time to keep from waking Mom and Dad. I could maneuver around this place blindfolded."

With that, she rounded the corner and disappeared. He could hear her footsteps as she moved through the house, and for a minute he just stood there, listening.

Bending down, he untied his boots and left them sitting by the door to dry. Next, he peeled off his shirt and let it drop on top of her jacket in the sink, followed by his heavy, rain-soaked jeans.

She probably wouldn't appreciate him walking around in his boxer shorts, but they were about the only stitch of dry clothing on his body at the moment, and he wanted to get that fire started before going upstairs to find something else to wear. Besides, they were nice boxers. Clean, new, navy blue with tiny white polka dots, and not a hole to be found. Lori had restocked his underwear drawer just last month. He hadn't much appreciated it at the time, but now he supposed he owed her a thank-you.

At the thought of Lori, guilt twisted through his gut. He hadn't even attempted to contact her since the night of Nick's wedding when she'd kicked him out of his own house. Worse yet, he didn't particularly miss her. He'd been perfectly content this week to stay at Nick's house, with Nick's sister.

With Beth.

As hard as he'd fought it all these years, he was attracted to her. Ha! That was the understatement of the century. He wanted her with a burning, seething, all-encompassing passion. And the more he tried to deny it, the more obsessed he became.

Even having her seven years ago hadn't dulled the desire coursing through his veins. Making love to her in the cab of his truck had only sharpened his feelings, turning her into a drug and him into a junkie.

Lori was a great girl, and he'd honestly tried to build a life with her. But now that Beth was back in town, now that this flame he'd held for her was flaring to life again, he realized that he'd only been lying to himself…and using Lori as a Band-Aid to treat a severed limb.

He heard a squeak and turned to see Beth coming down the stairs, a stack of fluffy white towels in her hands. She was wearing that short, sexy yellow nightie again, the equally short matching robe tied at her waist. Her wet hair was caught up at the back of her head with a silver clip.

Forcing himself to look away, he concentrated once again on getting a fire going in the living room hearth. Feeling more than seeing his way around, he unwrapped one of the pretreated starter bricks and struck a match, chagrined to notice that his hand was shaking.

Damn, she affected him. One whiff of her spicy perfume, one glimpse of her wide blue eyes and he started to sweat.

"Here you go."

She shook out a towel and draped it over his bare shoulders. His half-naked state didn't seem to bother her nearly as much as he'd expected.

The flames caught, filling the fireplace and beginning to throw flickering light and heat into the room. He stood, rubbing the towel over his close-cut hair and then drying his still-damp arms and chest. Beth had taken the clip out of her hair and was using her own towel to squeeze and separate the strands.

"I see you decided to go straight to the quick-dry method," she said, tipping her head in the direction of his bare body and boxer shorts.

"I didn't want to drip on your brother's hardwood floor. I can run upstairs and put on something else, if it bothers you."

He wasn't sure why he threw the offer out there and in that particular wording. It's what he'd intended from the start, but for some reason, he suddenly found himself wanting to know what her reaction would be to his remaining in this state of undress.

Would she ask him to go throw some clothes on, or be just as comfortable with him walking around half-nude as she was walking around that way herself? Because that slinky little nightgown she'd been wearing lately sure didn't leave much to the imagination.

"It doesn't bother me," she said breezily, walking to the couch and plopping down on one of the overstuffed cushions. She propped her feet on the coffee table and the seashell pink of her painted toenails winked in the flickering light of the fire.

"I've seen you and Nick both in a lot less." She grinned, looking at him from beneath lowered lashes. "Remember that time out at the lake when the two of you went skinny-dipping? You teased and badgered until I agreed to strip down and jump in with you, then you sneaked out and stole my clothes."

He chuckled at the memory, dropping the towel on the stone hearth to dry before taking a seat beside her on the sofa. He did remember that day, though he hadn't thought of it in years. "You cried so hard, we were afraid you'd drown."

"Which had no impact whatsoever on you two hooligans."

"No, but your screaming and threatening to walk home naked to tell your parents what we'd done certainly did."

"Yeah. So what did you do in response? You threw my clothes on the bank, then went running home without me."

"We had to get there before you did to make sure you wouldn't rat on us."

"Don't worry, I didn't. I still don't think Mom and Dad know about that incident."

"That's probably for the best. They'd think Nick and I were complete pervs."

She slanted a wicked glance in his direction. "What do you mean *were?*"

It took a second for the gibe to sink in, another for him to realize she was falling back on their old, teasing banter. Something she hadn't done in seven long years.

Before he could question why or tamp down his instinctive response, he narrowed his eyes, lowered his tone and said, "Low blow. Now you'll have to be punished."

Her brows lifted as understanding dawned, and she gave a shriek loud enough to rattle the pictures on the wall before trying to dart away. He grabbed her, snaking an arm around her waist before she got two inches off the couch, pulling her back against him. With his free hand, he dug into the tender flesh of her side and started to tickle.

"No! Aaack, stop! Connor, stop!"

She continued to scream and thrash, laughing uncontrollably. It was like old times. He used to tickle her like this when they were kids, and sometimes he and Nick would gang up on her.

Of course, she always got her revenge. By going to her folks and getting them grounded, but more often by putting garter snakes in their beds or itching powder in their shorts. She was nothing if not cruel and ingenious in her acts of vengeance.

Somehow, with all her wiggling, she got

twisted around so they were facing each other. Her breasts were pressed flat between them and he could feel her pebbled nipples digging into his bare chest through the thin fabric of her robe and nightie.

Though her knees nearly emasculated him more than once, the sensation of her smooth, silky legs gliding between his own sent signals to both his brain and nether regions, reminding him that he was definitely a man. And she was definitely a woman.

A woman he craved like a bear craved honey.

He stopped tickling, and her movements abruptly halted. She was panting for breath, the aftershocks of her laughter still rippling through her body.

Her face hovered above his, the damp tendrils of her hair hanging around them in dark spirals. Her eyes, which normally shone like bright, glittering sapphires, were now a deep, fathomless ocean blue. He read passion there, and longing…feelings he was more than willing to re-ciprocate.

He thought about kissing her, was lifting his head to do just that, when she leaned down and beat him to the punch. And what a punch it was. Right to the solar plexus. Her lips were warm and as soft as rose petals. Her fragrance invaded his senses, filling every pore.

He brought his hands up to frame her face and deepened the kiss, tasting her, absorbing her texture. Their tongues stroked, twined.

His fingers trailed through her hair, massaging her scalp, while she explored the expanse of his chest. She outlined the ridges of each pectoral muscle, his taut abdomen, brushing with her fin-gertips, clawing with her nails. He sucked in a ragged breath when she traced a path from his navel to the elastic waist of his boxers, stirring through the crisp hair there, sending shocks of electricity to every cell of his being.

She was smiling down at him, her lips puffy, her eyes half-lidded with desire.

"Do you want me to stop?" she asked, even as he felt the manicured tips of her fingernails worm their way between his fever-hot skin and the only piece of clothing that kept him from being indecent.

Beneath that material, though, he throbbed, straining for her touch. He wanted to beg her to keep going, to answer her question with a desperate *No, don't stop. Don't ever stop!*

But he couldn't take advantage of her, not again. If this was going to happen, if they were going to be together again, then he needed to know she wanted him as much as he wanted her. That there was nothing standing between them, nothing impairing her decision-making process.

Tucking a lock of hair behind her ear and keeping his hand on the nape of her neck, he asked, "How much did you have to drink tonight?"

She blinked, her eyes widening slightly as she

realized his question wasn't an intimate or suggestive one.

"Why? Do you think I'm drunk?" She spoke slowly and deliberately, but she didn't seem to be offended.

"I just want to be sure," he replied with measured care. So far, she hadn't slapped his face and stormed off, and if he was lucky, he wouldn't say anything to make her do either.

"I had three light beers over a four-hour period. I'm not drunk, Connor. I know exactly what I'm doing."

As soon as the words were out of her mouth, she recognized them as the truth. She might not be kissing him, caressing him for all the right reasons, but she still wanted him.

Heck, she'd wanted him for years. Even during that terrible time when she'd convinced herself she hated him, she'd never really managed to quash her desire for him. These past few days, trapped together in the same house, trying to keep their distance but only managing to strike sparks off one another, had only served to amplify that yearning.

What would it hurt to be with him one more—one last—time? It was obvious they were both charged and ready…willing and more than able. They were both adults, both unattached.

Sadly, she hadn't dated anyone significant in the last three or four years. In the past twelve to eighteen months, she hadn't dated *anyone.*

She was due, a little voice in her head whispered. But more than that, sleeping with Connor would get this low-level hum of longing out of her system and prove, once and for all, that she was over him.

Sleeping with him would not only scratch the itch that had developed by spending so much time together this past week, but also give her the closure she'd been needing ever since the first time they'd made love seven years ago.

Closure, yes. That's exactly what she needed. One night with Connor to extinguish the fire beating in her blood and exorcise any hard feelings still lingering between them. Then she would be able to fly back to L.A. without any of the ugly demons that had plagued her in the past.

She met his gaze, letting the backs of her fingers roam deeper beneath the waistband of his cute little polka-dot boxer shorts until she felt him twitch.

"I know exactly what I'm doing," she told him again, slowly and succinctly so he would have no doubt that she meant what she said. "Is that clear?"

"Yes, ma'am," was his strained but heartfelt response. "I'll never doubt your intentions again."

An amused smile stole across her lips. "See that you don't."

His eyes sparkled with devilish purpose, and then he was lifting himself up on his elbows, covering her mouth with his. He kissed her breathless, kissed her until she was purring with pleasure and leaning into him, wanting to melt, merge, become one with him.

He smelled fresh and clean, like the rain that had drenched them both. And he felt...he felt like heaven. Hard and firm, his muscles bunching beneath her touch. His chest was a work of art, chiseled, well defined, a master-piece. His legs rubbed against her own, the crisp hairs tickling, sending ripples of sensual aware-ness along her spine.

But it was his face that intrigued her, his face that could turn her on from across the room. The strong line of his jaw, sometimes stubbled with a sexy five o'clock shadow. The smooth, powerful brow that furrowed when he was annoyed or deep in thought. The straight, narrow nose with a tiny bump high on the bridge from the time he and Nick had gotten into a fight with some members of the opposing team after an away-from-home football game. And those gentle, brandy brown eyes that made her knees go weak with a single smoldering glance.

Connor's hands dragged through her hair, moving down her back and sides and around to the front of her waist. He untied the sash of her robe, causing the silky material to fall open, and then pushed it over her shoulders and down her arms.

As reluctant as she was to remove her fingers from the cozy nest of his boxers, she wanted to feel him, skin to skin. With a little shake, she let the airy material flutter to the floor.

She was in her nightgown and panties now, her arms, legs and back bare. Instead of being chilled, waves of heat washed over her, and she doubted they were from the fireplace.

Their breaths mingled and heaved as Connor's lips moved to her cheek, her jaw. His hands stroked the backs of her legs, his callused fingers sending shivers and shock waves straight to her core. He traced the lines behind her knees before straying higher, higher. He cupped her bottom, groaning when he discovered she was wearing a thong.

"You're so damn hot," he breathed against the taut column of her throat. "You make me crazy. You make me want to lick every inch of your luscious body. Suck your toes and fingers, your nipples and your lips. I want to carry you to my bed and never let you leave."

His hands on her buttocks and tongue on her collarbone had her senses reeling, but she struggled to absorb everything he was saying. The words warmed her all the way through and sent her level of arousal ratcheting up several notches.

"Since the bed upstairs is my brother's and it's quite a walk to your place," she asked in a ragged voice, "will the sofa do?"

"Oh, yeah, the sofa will do just fine."

His rough palms moved from her bottom to her hips, his fingers slipping under the thin straps holding her panties in place. With excruciating slowness, he tugged the scrap of fabric down, revealing her private places and leaving her open to the warm air circulating through the room. She lifted her legs, one and then the other, to help him remove the garment altogether.

At the same time, his mouth found and fastened upon one of her breasts, wetting her nipple through the material of her nightgown and causing the already pebbled tip to tighten even further. She arched her back, granting him better access, urging him on.

He played her body like a finely tuned instrument, knowing just where to touch and stroke, just how much pressure to use. Her head was spinning, blood pounding in her ears and pooling low in her belly, between her legs.

But something was missing. Connor was turned on, but not desperately, sweating and writhing beneath her. She wanted that. She wanted to touch and caress him, drive him to the brink of insanity and make him beg for more.

"Connor."

He continued to suckle and her inner muscles clenched.

"Connor."

"Hmm?"

He hummed in reply and the vibrations rippled straight to her core.

"Stop," she said, and was amazed at the speed in which he halted the motions of his tongue and hands. With this man, it appeared, no meant no.

He fell back on the couch, staring up at her. His hands still cradled her hips, his chest heaving with the pace of his breathing. She admired his control, considering how aroused she knew he was.

Leaning down, she gave him a long, lingering kiss. When she raised up again, his eyes flashed with bewilderment.

"I didn't mean stop-stop," she clarified rather than leave him in a state of confusion.

He moved his hands from beneath the hem of

her nightie, lightly tracing the underside of her forearms before linking the fingers of both hands. "What did you mean, then?"

She spread her legs, straddling his thighs to find a better balance as she hovered above him. Bringing their twined hands up, she used her lower body to perform a slow gyration atop his straining erection. Connor inhaled sharply, his lips rolling back to reveal gritted teeth.

"I meant…my turn."

Ten

As if her erotic declaration alone wasn't enough to set off miniature explosions throughout his bloodstream, Beth outdid herself by sitting up, crossing her arms in front of her and whipping her thin little wisp of a nightgown up and over her head in one quick movement. She tossed the garment aside, smiling down at him in all her naked glory.

She was magnificent. Smooth, pale flesh… glorious round breasts with small, plum-colored nipples, drawn tight with her arousal…

narrow, sculpted waist leading down to the flare of feminine hips…

More beautiful than a pinup girl, she was the sexiest thing he'd ever seen. And for tonight, at least, she was his.

He reached for her, but she stopped him.

"Ah, ah, ah." Catching his wrists, she pressed his arms above his head, flat to the cushions of the couch. "My turn, my rules. No touching from you—for now."

A short, sharp laugh burst past his lips. "I'm not sure I can abide by that rule. It might kill me."

"If it does," she murmured, sliding her hands back down his arms, into the sensitive dip of his armpits, to his chest, "I'll perform mouth-to-mouth and resuscitate you."

The very thought made his diaphragm constrict. "Only to have your wicked way with me again, no doubt."

She shrugged one slim shoulder. "A girl has to have her fun."

Thankfully, Beth was more than willing to include him in her idea of fun. Her nails raked down his chest, skimming his nipples, leaving twin paths of ecstasy in their wake. And then her hands jumped to her own body, running along the tops of her thighs, over her waist, to the globes of her breasts. She palmed their weight and held them up for his perusal.

Like he needed to be reminded of her mouth-watering assets. He'd already tasted one of those pert nipples—albeit through the material of her nightgown— and felt it bud against his tongue.

"Do you like what you see?"

Rather than answer her question, he rotated his hips, letting her feel his straining length between her legs, tenting the front of his boxers. "What do you think?"

She leaned forward, draping the upper half of her body along the upper half of his. He could feel her heat and wetness even through his shorts, and though he wouldn't have thought it possible a second earlier, he grew harder.

"I think…"

She placed an open-mouthed kiss to his neck. His senses were so heightened that he could hear the sandpaper scrape of her tongue against the underside of his whiskered jaw, like the raspy lick of a kitten.

"…you do."

Her mouth continued downward, leaving behind a path of moisture that all but sizzled on his overheated skin.

"I also think…"

She was at his pectorals now, flicking one tiny nipple before moving on to his rib cage.

"I like what *I* see."

The tip of her tongue swirled into his navel and the air seized in his lungs.

"I'm…glad," he managed in ragged pants.

"Connor?"

He couldn't breathe, which made it somewhat

difficult to answer. But what made it absolutely impossible was the sight of her teeth biting into and lifting the waistband of his boxer shorts. When he didn't answer, she released the elastic band with a snap. He barely felt the sting.

"I want you inside me."

Yes. Please. *Finally.*

Rules be damned. Jackknifing into a sitting position, he cupped her bare bottom and pulled her more fully onto his lap.

"Wrap your arms around my neck," he told her.

For once, she didn't argue. With a sensually contented grin, she threw herself onto him, plastering her breasts between them and looping her arms together in a near stranglehold.

Holding tight, he pushed to his feet. "Now wrap your legs around my waist."

"Yes, master."

One corner of his mouth quirked at her cheeky reply. "Behave or you'll have to be punished."

"Ooh, please don't hurt me," she cooed. "I promise I'll be good."

"But not too good."

"No, not too good," she agreed as he started walking.

She was stuck to him like a burr…just the way he liked it.

"Where are we going?"

"Kitchen. I left my pants in the sink."

"I thought we were getting *un*dressed. Why do you need your pants?"

They reached the kitchen and he propped her on the edge of the counter, freeing his hands to dig through his wet jeans. He got his wallet out of the rear pocket and found what he needed.

"Condom," he said, holding up the silver foil packet like it was an Olympic medal.

A look of startled realization flashed in her eyes. He guessed she hadn't given the need for protection much thought. But then, things had moved rather quickly once they'd decided being together this way was inevitable.

"Smart thinking." She ran her fingers from the nape of his neck up through his hair. "You keep one with you in case of sexual emergencies?" she teased.

"Yep. And there's a whole box upstairs, too. You never know when some hot babe is going to jump your bones."

She tipped her head to the side, studying him for a moment. "Men live in a constant state of fantastic optimism, don't they?"

He flashed her a wide grin. "Of course. And sometimes it pays off."

She smiled back at him. "So are you going to use that condom, or stand around talking about it?"

And just like that, his libido was flying full throttle again.

"I'm going to use it." He shucked off his boxers and tore the foil square open with his teeth at the same time. "Do you want to stay here or go back to the couch?"

She glanced around at the countertops and cleared kitchen table before meeting his gaze. "Here." She pulled him closer with both her arms and legs. "Now. Hurry."

"Be careful what you wish for, sweetheart." He was already full to bursting, aching for her. Too much more and it would be over before it began.

Making short work of covering himself with the thin layer of protection, he grabbed her up and kissed her. Her nails raked across his back, her ankles locked over his buttocks.

While their mouths meshed and their breaths mingled, he lifted her from the counter and carried her to the table, laying her on the flat surface like a delectably erotic feast.

She sighed and arched toward him, and he took the opportunity to nuzzle her throat, her chest. He circled one breast, then the other, purposely avoiding the straining peaks and leaving her wanting.

With his lips on the soft, flat plane of her belly, he nudged the tip of his throbbing erection against her warm, wet opening. She writhed, trying to get closer, and he was so wildly aroused that he knew he couldn't tease either of them any longer. He wanted her, needed her, had to have her right that moment or die.

Surging forward, he buried himself inside her to the hilt, meeting her mouth and swallowing her gasp of delight.

She felt like heaven, wet and hot and tight around him. He could have stayed that way forever, nestled in the cradle of her thighs, but she flexed her hips, urging him on, and his desperate libido took over.

They moved together, thrusting, driving, fighting for air as their muscles strained and the blood pounded in their veins.

Beth bit her bottom lip to keep from crying out

at the sensations washed over her, but she kept her eyes open, watching Connor move above her. Her stomach quivered, her tender inner muscles clenching and releasing around him as he filled her.

She held him close with her arms and legs wound around him, wanting to bring him as deep as possible, to become one with him. The soft, springy hair on his chest abraded her breasts, sending a Morse code of awareness down to her core.

Moaning her pleasure, she nipped at his earlobe with her teeth. She could feel the pressure building, release just beyond her grasp, and she reached for it, straining, striving, lifting to meet every pounding drive of his hips.

"Faster, Connor. Please."

"Yes."

He hooked his arms under her knees, pushing them even closer to her body to grant him better access as he increased his pace, and within seconds they both came, completion washing over them in wave after wave of the most intense pleasure she'd ever experienced. The tremors wracking her body went on and on as he thrust once, twice more and then fell still above her.

His weight draped across her torso, heavy, but in an intimate, comforting way. Her fingertips drew nonsensical designs on his sweat-slick back and her lips were tipped up in what she knew must be a goofy grin.

Raising his tousled head, he stared down at her, satisfaction glittering in his dark brown eyes.

"You're smiling," he said.

"I know."

His fingers brushed over the hair at her temples. "You look amazing."

"I feel pretty amazing." She clutched at him where he rested inside her and felt him begin to stiffen again. "So do you."

He raised a brow. "Again?"

"I'm ready when you are." She flexed once more, just in case he had any doubts.

"Well, I'll be damned."

He scooped her up from the table, keeping them connected, and swung around, heading out of the kitchen.

"You sure do move around a lot," she told him, hanging on and enjoying the jostling of their lower bodies with each step he took. "Now where are we going?"

"Upstairs for more condoms. We may even make it into a bed this time."

"Mmm, making love in a bed. What a novel idea."

He chuckled, slapping her bare bottom. "Don't be sarcastic. If you hadn't been in such an all-fired hurry, we might have made it there the first time."

"Oh, sure. Blame the poor defenseless naked woman being carted around like a sack of potatoes."

A second later, he cracked his shin into a piece of furniture and swore.

It was Beth's turn to laugh. "Are you okay?"

"I'll live," he replied through gritted teeth, rubbing absently at the bruised spot before continuing.

"Need a flashlight?" she asked sweetly, throwing his earlier words back at him.

"Very funny. Now be quiet while I concentrate on getting upstairs *without* maiming myself."

"I won't say another word," she promised in a hushed whisper.

Instead, she brushed her lips along his cheekbone to his ear, where she sucked the fleshy lobe into her mouth and bit down gently with her teeth. He grunted, stumbling over the next step.

"You're killing me," he grumbled. "I hope you know that."

She grinned, but didn't respond. After all, she'd agreed to be quiet.

At the top of the stairs, he tripped again, letting

her fall to the landing and following her down. His body covered hers as he kissed her, releasing every ounce of passion and frustration that had built up in the last few minutes. When he pulled away, they were both breathing heavily.

"Enough is enough," he said, slipping out of her.

She moaned in disappointment, already missing the feel of him inside her. But then he stood, scooping her into his arms, and made a beeline for the master bedroom.

Reaching the bed, he dropped her in its center, and without a word crossed to the dresser. The mattress hadn't stopped bouncing by the time he returned, old condom gone and a box of new condoms in his hand.

He removed a single packet and tore it open, covering himself before he climbed onto the bed beside her.

"Where were we?" he wanted to know.

"Right about here." She lifted her leg to drape over his hip and ran her fingers up and down his bare, bulging bicep. The tip of his masculinity pressed against her slick opening, seeking entrance, and she was more than willing to let him in.

As he sank into her and her arms wrapped around him, drawing him closer, Beth sighed with contentment. She was getting exactly what she wanted: one night with Connor Riordan.

It would all evaporate like mist in the morning, but for tonight, he was hers.

Beth's eyes fluttered open what must have been hours later. The room was still dark, but a hint of early-morning light filtered through the blinds from outside. The rain had stopped sometime during the night, and for long minutes, she lay there, unmoving, listening to the sounds of birdsong.

She was cuddled up to Connor, her back to his front, with the blankets pulled up to their chests. Beneath the sheets, his arm circled her waist and her arm ran along his, her palm covering the back of his hand so that their fingers linked.

She felt warm and safe and never wanted to move. A part of her even wanted to roll over and coax Connor awake with kisses and a gentle caress.

But she knew she couldn't. She'd promised herself one night to wash him from her system, to prove she was over him, and that one night was now passed.

It was time to start distancing herself, and the sooner she did that, the sooner things would get back to normal.

Freeing her fingers, she loosened the sheets on her side of the bed and slid her feet out, then carefully slipped out from under his hold. She tiptoed across the hall to her bedroom, dressing in the first items of clothing she found, the low-riding jeans and cotton top she'd worn yester-day to paint.

She used the hallway bathroom, planning to

go downstairs and start a pot of coffee. But as she passed the open doorway of the nursery, the weak rays of morning sunlight flooding through the curtainless windows, spilling across the newly refinished floor, stopped her in her tracks.

Even without furniture, the room was beautiful. Nick and Karen were going to love it. Any baby would be lucky to grow up here, especially knowing his aunt and "uncle" had put so much time and love into the renovations.

So why did just looking at the fresh paint and unopened rolls of sea-creatures border paper make her sad?

Letting her fingertips trace over the carved wooden doorjamb and new seafoam-colored walls, she stepped inside. She could picture the nursery exactly as it would be when it was finished, complete with a crib, changing table and rocking chair. Maybe even a bassinet for when the baby was still tiny and newborn.

She imagined her brother and his wife

bringing their first child home from the hospital…Nick rocking the baby while it slept; Karen sitting there, breast-feeding.

But suddenly, it wasn't Karen rocking Beth's little niece or nephew. It was she, rocking *her* child. Her baby with Connor.

She'd never seen their child, having miscarried so early in her pregnancy, but she had no problem now making out every detail of her baby's features. The tiny little dot of a nose, the puffy baby cheeks, the delicate rosebud lips puckering in sleep.

A sob escaped her and she backed against the wall, feeling the impact of the loss like a musket ball to the stomach. She covered her mouth with her hand and sank to the floor, feeling tears streaming down her face.

Except for a lingering resentment toward Connor, she really thought she'd gotten over the emotional upheaval of the miscarriage years ago. How ironic to discover that while she'd managed to forgive Connor only days before for any part he did or didn't play in the events of seven years ago, it was the actual loss that still hung so heavily on her heart and soul.

It was so easy to envision what her life might have been if she hadn't lost the baby. If she'd remained pregnant and found the courage to tell Connor that they were going to be parents, she knew exactly what would have happened. They'd have gotten married and found some-where to live right here in Crystal Springs, where they could be near her mom and dad.

And they would have been happy. She'd have finished school eventually and gone on to get her law degree...or maybe she'd have been happy as a stay-at-home mom. She and Connor might have had a couple more kids, her days filled with running carpools, cooking dinners and throwing birthday parties the envy of the neighborhood.

And as successful, as happy as she'd been with

her life in L.A., she knew she would have been equally—maybe even more—happy staying in her own hometown as a wife and mother.

But only to Connor and his children.

How had life gone so terribly wrong? She'd had such big hopes and dreams in high school and her first years of college, all of which had come crashing down in a matter of weeks. Whether it was the miscarriage or Connor's failure to call her after the night they were together didn't seem to matter now. None of it did. It was just life, with all its ups and downs, joys and disappointments.

She'd made mistakes along the way, too. Not telling Connor the truth from the very beginning possibly being one of the biggest.

Before she went back to California, she would be sure to rectify that. It wouldn't be easy, she knew, but it had to be done. He deserved to know, and she deserved to spend the rest of her life with a clear conscience.

They could never go back, never reclaim what was already lost, but they could move forward and continue to be friends instead of avoiding each other like the plague.

Of course, after last night, that might not be entirely possible. But getting past secret-sex guilt had to be simpler than getting past secret-pregnancy guilt and seven years of lies.

Taking a deep breath, Beth wiped her eyes and climbed to her feet. To her surprise, she felt relieved and more comfortable in her own skin than she had in ages. It wasn't just the crying jag that cleansed her spirit, she realized, but her decision to come clean with Connor. What a crushing weight that had been to carry around all these years.

She was still sniffing, drying her face with the hem of her shirt when a floorboard squeaked and she lifted her head to find Connor standing on the other side of the doorway. He'd pulled on a clean pair of boxer shorts, but was otherwise

gloriously naked. The sun spilling through the
windows was brighter now, turning his legs and
chest a golden bronze.

"Are you all right?" he asked, brows drawing
together in concern. "What's wrong?"

She made one last swipe at her face, even
though she knew it was too late to hide the fact
that she'd been crying. He'd already noticed her
tear-stained cheeks and red, swollen nose.

"Nothing, I'm fine," she said. And then she
shook her head. "No, that's not entirely true."

Reaching out, she took his hand and pulled
him farther into the room. "Connor, there's
something I need to tell you."

His face blanched, his grip on her hand tight-
ening as he sensed it was bad news. "Okay."

She took a deep breath and dived in, knowing
if she didn't, she might never get it out. "I never
told you this, but seven years ago, when we slept
together after that football game, I got pregnant."

His expression didn't change, but she felt his

entire body turn to stone. Whether that meant he was furious with her or merely digesting the information, she pressed on.

"I didn't tell you, and I should have. I think I would have, early on, if you had ever called or come to see me."

She held up her free hand, not to ward off any arguments he might make, but to keep herself from traveling down that tired, well-worn path.

"I'm not blaming you or saying you did anything wrong. We both made mistakes seven years ago, and if we had it to do over again, I'm sure we would do things a bit differently. I'm just telling you this because…" She lowered her eyes and licked her dry lips. "You deserve to know. And I'm tired of keeping it a secret, tired of being mad at you for something you weren't even aware of."

"I don't understand." His voice rasped, his Adam's apple bobbing as he swallowed hard, searching for words. "If you were pregnant, where's the baby?"

She blinked, caught off guard by the question. She'd been expecting a barrage of anger, a furious *why didn't you tell me?* Instead, she realized she hadn't shared with him the most important part of what had happened all those years ago.

"I'm sorry, Connor. I should have told you right away," she said, her own throat threatening to close on her. "I lost the baby."

For long minutes, he held her gaze, barely blinking, barely breathing. "I don't know what to say," he finally forced out.

"It's all right, you don't have to say anything. I just…don't want you to hate me. I spent a lot of time carrying this pain around with me, and even though I think you have the right to know everything that happened back then, I don't want you to make the same mistake now."

"I wish you'd told me. As soon as you found out."

She nodded in agreement. "I know. I wish I

had, too. But I was young and scared, and I hadn't heard from you since that night."

His fingers clamped around hers. "If I'd known, I would have done the right thing. I never would have let you go through that alone."

One corner of her mouth turned up in a bitter-sweet half smile. "I know you wouldn't have. And I appreciate it."

They stood there for several more seconds, each at a loss as to what else needed to be said. Beth hoped her confession would ease her conscience, but she also hoped Connor wouldn't dwell too long on the past… the way she had.

"I'm flying back to California tomorrow," she said after the silence had dragged on for a full minute. Running her palm over his stubbled cheek, she added, "Thank you for last night, and thank you for that night seven years ago. Despite everything, I really am glad you were my first."

With that, she pulled her hand from his and stepped around him, out of the room.

Eleven

Connor stood in stunned silence long after Beth walked away. Minutes or even hours might have passed, he wasn't sure which. And he didn't care.

He heard Beth's footsteps as she paced down the hall, heard her moving around in her bedroom, likely packing. And he wanted to chase after her, he really did. But his feet seemed glued to the floor, and his brain refused to function past the bomb she'd just dropped on him.

They'd made a baby together and he'd never

known it. She'd lost that baby and he'd never known it. The ramifications of those facts whirled through his head like a tornado.

He thought he'd been an idiot seven years ago for letting things get out of hand with her in the first place, but now he *knew* he was an idiot for not checking on her afterward. For not calling to see if she was all right, both physically and emotionally. For not driving up to the university to be sure there'd been no consequences from his lapse of judgment.

He'd been young, sure, but old enough to take responsibility for his actions, especially where Beth was concerned. If anything, he owed her more courtesy and respect than other girls because they'd grown up together, practically as family.

A baby. He couldn't believe it. He'd fought his attraction to her for so long, and the one time he'd given in, he'd gotten her pregnant. Worse, she hadn't felt comfortable enough to come to him when she'd found out.

He had no one but himself to blame for that. The signals he'd been sending her since their early teens must have confused her beyond reason. Between treating her like a pesky little sister, then casting longing glances in her direction when he thought she wasn't looking, she probably hadn't known which end was up. And then he hadn't even had the courtesy to contact her the day after taking her virginity.

What a heel! What a dumb, selfish jerk! He'd walked away seven years ago, thinking they could forget, pretend that night hadn't happened.

But she hadn't been able to pretend or forget, had she? She'd been young, alone and unexpectedly pregnant by a man who not only didn't call her after sleeping with her, but did his level best to avoid being alone with her any time she came home for a visit.

To top it all off, she'd also been alone when she miscarried. He couldn't imagine how horrible that must have been for her. The fear, the pain, the sadness. No wonder she'd treated him like a particularly foul species of vermin whenever he was around. He deserved every ounce of her disdain—that and more.

And he didn't have a clue how to make up for any of it...or if he ever could.

His head was still spinning when Beth peeked around the corner and caught his attention. She wore her work clothes, the jeans and top they'd bought during their trip for nursery supplies.

"I called the airline," she said softly. "Now that the storm has passed, flights are back on track. My plane for L.A. leaves tomorrow afternoon. I was wondering if you'd drive me over to say goodbye to Mom and Dad in the morning, then drop me off at the airport."

He nodded, not quite able to manage actual words yet. His throat felt as though someone had their hands around his neck, squeezing, *squeezing* until he couldn't breathe.

A beat passed before she murmured a quiet thank-you and returned to her room.

God, how was he going to resolve this? How could he assimilate everything that had happened, everything she'd told him, and put it right? And if she was leaving tomorrow, did he even have time?

He didn't want her to leave again, fly all the way across the country, with this between them. Possibly forever. They'd spent the last seven years feeling awkward and avoiding each other…he didn't want to slip back into that strained behavior simply because he was fool enough to let her get on a plane before they'd cleared the air.

But how he was going to do that, he hadn't a clue.

Connor sat in his truck at the curb while Beth said goodbye to her parents. He'd driven her over earlier, expecting a quick visit before taking her the rest of the way to the airport, but Helen and Patrick had been so happy to see their daughter again and so sorry to see her go, that they'd insisted Beth and Connor sit down with them for a nice lunch of cold-meat sandwiches and fruit salad.

It had reminded him of old times, but he'd still felt uncomfortable. Helen and Patrick Curtis had always treated him like one of their own, even though he'd been nothing more than the scruffy foster child from across the street. He'd been a troublemaker, but they'd looked beyond that to the boy beneath who was desperate for a family, a place to belong, and for someone to love him. They'd given him all that and more, and continued to into his adulthood.

He would do anything for them, which included *not* betraying their trust by taking advantage of their only daughter.

But it was a little late to avoid that trap, wasn't it? He'd not only slept with Beth the night before last, he'd taken her virginity seven years ago, leaving her pregnant and alone. Thankfully, those particular gems of information hadn't come up during lunch.

He also hadn't thought of a single solution for settling things between them. She was saying her farewells to her mom and dad on the front lawn, then he would drop her off for her flight to California. Never to be seen again.

At least not for a good long while. She didn't come home very often. And she most especially wouldn't come home just to see him.

Dammit. What was he going to do?

The passenger door opened, breaking into his troubled thoughts. She climbed in beside him and he noticed the telltale glimmer in her eyes.

"You okay?"

She turned to look at him, sniffing to hold back tears. "Yeah, I just…never expected it to be so hard to leave." Digging in her purse for a tissue, she dabbed at her nose. "I've been back other times, but it's never felt this bad to take off again."

"Maybe that's because this time felt more like coming home."

The sudden leeching of color from her face told him he'd hit a little too close to the bone. But instead of responding, she glanced out the window, waving to her parents, who still stood in the yard. He took the hint and started the truck, lifting his own hand to Helen and Patrick as they pulled away from the curb.

The ride to the airport passed in silence. Not uncomfortable, just…quiet. He tried a dozen times to broach the subject of their relation-ship—past and present. The words swirled in his head, forming and then fading away before they reached the tip of his tongue.

He wanted to punch the steering wheel in frustration. Why couldn't he figure out what to say to her?

Pulling into the airport parking area, he shut off

the pickup's engine and got out to unload her luggage from the truck bed. They made their way into the terminal. Beth checked her suitcase at the desk, and they walked together toward security.

Before reaching the metal detectors, she stopped, twisting slowly on the sole of her black pumps to lift her head and meet his gaze.

She was wearing a black power suit that made her look every inch the competent lawyer. Black slacks, black jacket, with a burnt-orange blouse underneath to brighten things up. Small gold hoops adorned her ears, a thin gold chain spark-ling around her neck beneath the collar of her blouse. If he didn't know better, he'd think she was on her way to a multimillion-dollar contract negotiation. And he had no doubt she'd win every argument she made.

Her blue eyes shone up at him and his gut clenched at her never-ending beauty. Not just on the outside, but on the inside, too. She was every-thing he'd ever wanted in a woman, yet they were destined to revolve around each other, never stopping long enough to figure out what was really going on. Like asteroids, flying through space, occasionally crashing into one another before shooting off again in the opposite direction.

Tucking a strand of loose hair behind her ear, she said, "You don't have to go the rest of the way with me. I'll be fine, and I know you must have better things to do with your day than sitting around waiting for my plane to board."

He shoved his hands into the front pockets of his jeans, rocking back on the heels of his work boots. "Are you sure?"

She offered him a kind smile. "I'm sure."

Reaching out, she brushed her hand down the length of his arm, her heat warming him even through the light blue material. "Thank you for all you did while I was home this time. We may have started out on the wrong foot, but it was nice of you to drive me around when I needed it."

"No problem." A beat passed while he attempted to bring one of his earlier speeches to the forefront of his mind. Instead, all he could think to say was, "It was good to see you again."

"You, too, Connor."

"I'm sorry about everything, Beth Ann," he blurted out.

He would have said more, but she raised a hand, covering his mouth with two soft, manicured fingers.

"I told you, it's all right." She let her fingertips fall from his lips, landing on his forearm instead. "I'm glad we're friends again. I've missed you."

His mouth went stone dry at that and he could have sworn he felt tears prickling behind his eyes.

"Call me sometime," she added.

And then, before he could clear his throat to respond, she shifted the strap of her purse higher on her shoulder, offered him one final, friendly smile, and turned to leave.

He watched her pass through security, walking off toward her gate without a backward glance. His stomach churned, his palms sweating as he realized it was too late. She was gone. He'd missed his chance.

He stood there for several more minutes, watching after her—wishing she would come back into view, that he could relive their conversation and do it right instead of letting her slip away before he'd cleared his mind and his conscience.

With a heavy sigh, he let his chin drop to his chest dejectedly. That's it, it was over.

He wasn't even sure what he'd hoped to accomplish, other than making sure she knew how sorry he was for not being there for her seven years ago, for not being around to learn about the baby or help her through the miscarriage.

But the single resounding thought looping through his mind as he left the airport and headed for his truck wasn't that he'd failed to call her after they slept together the first time, or that he'd never known he was almost a father.

It was that he'd lost her.

A week later, Connor stood in the doorway of the finished nursery, his shoulder against the jamb as he studied the ocean-blue walls, the sea-creatures wallpaper border, the billowy white curtains. He'd put together a crib for the corner and a changing table for the far wall, and even installed a shelf above the table for powder, wipes, stuffed animals, whatever.

He'd done it all on his own, without Beth's guidance and feminine touch. And he'd missed it, dammit. He'd missed her.

Luckily, a woman at the store had pointed him in the right direction and helped him pick out some of the items. But just in case, he'd kept the receipts so Nick and Karen could return or exchange anything they didn't care for.

They'd gotten back from their honeymoon

yesterday, and he'd reluctantly shown them the room. He'd wanted it to be a surprise, wanted to do something special for his best friend and his new wife and child. And he thought he'd accomplished that. Nick had been shocked at the transformation of his old bedroom, and Karen had burst into tears, sniffing and laughing happily as she moved around touching every stuffed animal, admiring each and every detail.

He was glad his friends liked the room, but his own pleasure in their reactions had been dampened by Beth's absence. It had been *their* project, not just his. She should have been there to see her brother's face and receive one of Karen's bone-crushing hugs.

He could picture her standing on a stepladder, affixing the border paper to the top of the wall, glue in her hair, paper unrolling out of control. He could hear her laughter as she struggled to keep her balance, see the gentle curve of her bottom beneath those low-riding jeans she'd worn while they worked, and imagined himself walking up behind her, running his hands over her legs and derriere until she gave up on her task and turned to kiss him instead.

Skipping ahead a few years, his brain decided to take a sharp detour into what their lives would be if they actually got together, if they married and started a family of their own. They would have a nursery just like this someday…or at least similar. Beth would bring her own unique sense of style to the decorating process, so their child could definitely look forward to something more exciting than clowns or teddy bears.

She would rock their babies to sleep while he watched from the doorway, then they would both put the child to bed and stand at the side of the crib, hand in hand, gazing down at the miracle they'd created.

God, he wanted that, he thought, pinching the bridge of his nose where a headache was starting to throb.

So why did he only figure that out now, when it was already too late?

Distracted by his daydreams and self-flagellation, Connor didn't hear Nick come up behind him until his friend slapped a hand on his shoulder and squeezed.

"Admiring your handiwork?"

"Yeah," he said, returning Nick's grin, even though it wasn't close to his true train of thought.

"I still can't believe you and Beth did all this. I wish she'd stuck around long enough for Karen and me to thank her." He gave Connor's shoulder another squeeze. "Thank you, too, man. You can't know what this means to us."

Connor inclined his head. "You deserve it. Both of you. I hope you'll be happy together for a long, long time."

Pushing away from the wall, he dug into his hip pocket and pulled out a small stack of paper slips. "Here. In case you want to return anything."

Nick took the receipts, shoving them into his

own pocket, but said, "Are you kidding me? After a honeymoon in Hawaii, I thought I'd be lucky if Karen didn't start begging me to build a dolphin enclosure in the backyard. Now she's got this to remind her. Good call, buddy."

Taking a deep breath, Connor swallowed hard. "It wasn't my idea, it was your sister's."

Maybe it was the tone of his voice or the tension in every fiber of his body, but Nick shifted to face him, leaning back against the opposite side of the doorway and crossing his arms over his chest.

"Something going on between you and my sister that I should know about?"

Connor's spine snapped carpenter's-level straight. He took a step back, meeting his friend's serious expression, and the denial leaped immediately to his lips. "No, of course not." He paused for a single kettledrum beat of his heart. "Why do you ask?"

"Come on," Nick scoffed with a wry chuckle.

"You think I haven't noticed the way you two look at each other? The sparks that go off whenever you're together? It's been going on since we were kids."

"I—" He gave a strangled laugh. "I don't know what you're talking about."

"What's the big deal?" his friend wanted to know. "You like each other. You might as well see where it goes. And if it works out, all the better." He shrugged. "You're practically family already. I'd like nothing more than to be able to call you my brother-in-law, as well as my best friend."

Connor's chest grew tight, a ball of emotion the size of his fist blocking his airway. He strained for breath, fought to keep the tears from gathering in the corners of his eyes.

"You're sure?" he finally managed, the words scraping like sandpaper past his dry lips while his head spun. "You wouldn't mind if I dated Beth?"

"Hell, no," Nick responded, landing a playful punch to his bicep. "Marry her, for all I care. Just make sure you're good to her," he warned with a pointed finger, "or I'll have to kick your ass."

He might have laughed, if the ground weren't still shifting dangerously beneath his feet.

"What about your parents?" he made himself ask. "Don't you think they'd mind if the foster kid from across the street started messing around with their daughter?"

Nick grew serious, his brows drawing together, twin lines of concern bracketing his mouth. "You're the only one who ever thought of yourself as a foster child. The rest of us just thought of you as Connor…our friend, and another member of the Curtis clan. Mom and Dad would probably love it if you and Beth hooked up. Even if they didn't think much of it at first, they'd be fine as long as Beth was happy. That's all they really want, anyway…and I don't mind telling you they don't think she is right now. Happy, I mean."

"No?"

He shook his head. "California is too far away. We hardly ever hear from her, she works too hard, and she pops antacids like they're candy. We're worried about her. Mom, Dad and I would like nothing better than for her to come to her senses and move back to Crystal Springs."

Connor's hands were clenching and unclenching at his sides, the shock of Nick's admission warring with the need to rush out and track down Beth. "You think she would?"

"I don't know," Nick said carefully. "Depends on what she had to come home to."

He met his friend's compassionate blue eyes, so much like his sister's, and blurted out the secret he'd been keeping for more than ten years. "I'm in love with her. I'm in love with your sister."

A wide grin broke out across Nick's face. "Yeah? She feel the same way?"

"I don't know," he answered honestly. And that suddenly terrified him more than the idea that her parents might not approve.

"Well, what are you standing here for?" Nick challenged, giving Connor a less-than-subtle nudge in the ribs with his elbow. "Go find out."

Taking a deep breath, he squared his shoulders and nodded in agreement. "Yeah, I think I need to go find out."

He started down the hall, determined now.

"Call if you need anything," Nick shouted after him.

He lifted a hand to wave in acknowledgment, but didn't slow his steps. He was on a mission, to hunt down the woman he loved.

And make damn sure she loved him back.

Twelve

Beth finished making notations on one of her clients' latest contracts, pleased to get the review out of the way before her lunch appointment.

She'd been playing catch-up ever since returning from Ohio. The scheduled time away would have been difficult enough to work around, but now she had to go out and schmooze one of Danny's more difficult clients because he was at home with his sick son and she'd promised to cover his appointments until he returned.

Her stomach pitched and she automatically reached for the roll of antacids she kept next to the sticky-note dispenser on her desk. Funny that she hadn't needed the medication even once while she'd been home.

Home. As hard as she'd tried to deny it, she did still think of Crystal Springs as home. Her family was there, and if she was brave enough to admit it, so was her heart.

Tamping down that thought, she bit into another tablet, grinding it between her teeth.

So she hadn't needed ulcer or migraine medicine while she'd been in Ohio. The same could probably be said if she'd spent a week in Jamaica. Being away from work was bound to reduce her stress level, regardless of what occurred during her vacation.

Setting the contract folder aside until she could discuss the proposed changes with her client, she walked to the bathroom to check her hair and makeup. She was unlocking the bottom drawer of her desk to retrieve her purse when the intercom buzzed.

"Yes, Nina?"

"There's a gentleman here to see you, Miss Curtis."

She frowned. Nina usually gave her adequate warning of exactly who was seeking an appointment and why. And she certainly didn't have time today for unexpected visitors or potential new clients.

"Who is it?" she asked.

"He…would rather not say."

With an annoyed sigh, she checked her watch. "Fine," she said shortly. "But please explain to him that I'm on my way out and only have a couple of minutes. If he needs more time than that, he'll have to make an appointment."

"This won't take long."

At the sound of his voice, her heart stuttered to a halt in her chest, then picked up again at the speed of a racing freight train.

She hadn't heard the door open, but she heard it click quietly closed, and forced herself to lift her head, to meet his gaze.

He looked good. Lord, how could she think he looked better than he had the last time she'd seen him, when that was only a week and a half ago?

But even though it defied logic, he was more handsome than ever, standing across the room in his faded denims, well-worn boots and jean jacket open to reveal a red-plaid button-down shirt. His face was clean-shaven, his short hair combed and neat. His brown eyes burned into her, narrowed with determination.

"Connor," she said breathlessly. "What are you doing here?"

"I forgot to tell you something before you left."

Her eyes went wide in astonishment. "So you climbed on a plane and flew out here? You couldn't just pick up the phone?"

"Nope."

He took a step toward her and her knees

threatened to buckle. She held herself upright with her palms pressed flat to the top of the desk, when what she really wanted to do was fall backward into her big, wheeled leather chair. But she was too curious about why he'd traveled cross-country to see her, and she didn't want to be sitting down when the answer came.

"All right." The words came out strangled and she swallowed hard before continuing. "What did you want to tell me?"

He moved forward another dogged pace, his thumbs hooked under the edges of his pant pockets, and her stomach fluttered wildly with anticipation.

"I love you."

She blinked, not sure she'd heard him correctly. But she must have, because the air in her lungs dried up and her ears began to buzz. Surely her body wouldn't have such a strong physical reaction to a more benign statement.

Lifting a hand to cover her pounding heart, she

leaned heavily against the side of the desk and licked her parched lips. "Did you just say—"

"I love you."

This time, he came around the desk, grasping her by the tops of her arms and pulling her up to her full height. She craned her neck to meet his potent gaze.

"I'll say it as many times as it takes to make you believe," he told her with a slight shake. "I love you, Beth. I was crazy to let you walk away from me at the airport without telling you. I was crazy to pretend it wasn't true seven years ago…hell, ten years ago when I started to notice you less as my best friend's sister and more as a girl I wanted to go out with."

She wanted to weep, wanted to throw her arms around his neck and kiss him with all the love and passion in her soul. But she'd been hurt before. Gotten her hopes up, only to have them smash back down, lying broken on the ground at her feet. She couldn't go through that again.

"Why…" She cleared her throat and tried again. "Why are you telling me this now?"

"Because I've been a fool long enough. And I finally had a conversation with Nick that I probably should have had a decade ago. I told him I was in love with you, even though I was scared to death he'd bloody my nose for it…or worse, tell me to get lost. Tell me he wasn't my friend anymore, that I wasn't welcome near your family ever again."

His eyes closed for a brief moment, then opened again, myriad emotions visible in their coffee brown depths. "That's always been my biggest fear. That I'd do something stupid to screw up what I had with you guys. I was just this scruffy foster kid who landed across the street from the greatest family in the world. You treated me like one of your own, but I knew that wasn't true. I knew you and Nick belonged, and I was an interloper. One mistake, and you'd realize what a fraud I really was, and it would all come crashing down around my ears."

"Oh, Connor." The protective walls surrounding her crumbled and she lifted a hand to feather through the soft hair at his temple. "We never thought of you that way."

A crooked smile creased the corner of his mouth. "I guess I know that…now. But I didn't when we were teenagers, when I started to have feelings for you that I didn't think your folks would appreciate."

"Is that why you started to avoid me in high school? And why you never called after we slept together the night of the big football game?"

He nodded ruefully. "I was petrified about messing things up with you, that if your parents knew I had the hots for their daughter, they'd run me out of town on a rail."

"They never—"

"Yeah, your brother sort of convinced me of that the other day. After I told him how I really feel about you." His hands slipped down her arms, sliding around her waist. "He and Karen loved the nursery, by the way. I finished it up as best I could. She cried, and he was speechless for a good three minutes…which is the longest I think I've ever seen him go without having something to say."

Pulling her close, he lowered his head and rested his brow against hers. "I wish you had been there with me when I showed them the room, though. I want you with me always, Beth. I've been an idiot for so long…I don't want to go on making the same mistakes with you. If you're willing to give me a chance, I'll do everything in my power to make you happy. And if your family doesn't approve…"

She felt him swallow, felt his fingers flex at her back.

"Well, then, I'm sorry, but I'm not going to love you any less, and I'm not going to waste any more time hiding my feelings. If they reject me, so be it. But they'll have a hard time getting rid of me, considering I'll hopefully be married to their little girl by then."

Beth jerked back, studying him with a rapidly beating pulse and a yearning building in her chest like a tidal wave. "What are you saying?" she asked, her voice rasping with a thick mix of emotion and skepticism.

He glared at her in mock irritation. "What am I saying? What do you think I'm saying? Only the same thing I've been telling you for the past ten minutes. I love you. I've always loved you. I want to marry you, and have children with you, and grow old with you."

She shook her head, still not quite sure her ears weren't playing tricks on her. Oh, she wanted to believe, so badly. But the logical side of her brain kept insisting he couldn't have changed his mind about her in such a short time…that if he didn't feel this way when they were in bed together, he couldn't possibly feel this way now.

And yet, he'd gotten on a plane—which she happened to know was not his favorite mode of transportation—and flown across the country to see her, to look her in the eye and confess his love for her.

To ask her to marry him!

"I'm sorry about the baby," he said, apparently taking her silence for indecision. "I'm sorry about how I acted after the first time we made love. I couldn't have been a bigger cad if I'd tried. And I'm sorry—so much sorrier than you'll ever know—for not being there when you lost the baby. I would have loved to raise a child with you. Even if I'd been afraid your father would come after me with a shotgun for taking advantage of his little girl, I still would have done the right thing. I still would have wanted to be with you."

Raising his warm, callused hands to her face, he brushed her cheeks, then ran his fingers through the curls on either side of her head. "I want to make more babies with you, if you're agreeable."

His fingers tightened in her hair, but he didn't let go. "I'll understand if you don't want to leave L.A. Your life is here now. I don't expect you to just up and abandon your job and partner." He drew a deep breath, nostrils flaring. "I had a lot of time to figure this out on the plane, and I think I can sell my share of the company to Nick. We're making enough now that he can buy me out, then I can move out here with you. I don't know what I'll do for work, but I'll come up with something. I can always get a construction job, or—"

She covered his mouth with her hand, a smile tugging at the corners of her lips. "Connor, stop."

The smile broke into a full-fledged grin, and she couldn't hold back the laughter bubbling up from her belly. Was it any wonder she loved this man? Beyond his kindness and compassion and his adorable rear end, he was selfless. Once he made up his mind to love someone, there wasn't anything he wouldn't do for them. And she counted herself oh-so-lucky to be on the short list of people he cared that much about.

"There's something I forgot to tell *you* back at the airport, too."

She felt his chest hitch in nervous anticipation.

"What's that?" he asked warily.

"I love you." The tension drained from his body in a rush, and she rose on her toes to press her mouth to his. "I always have, you know that. I wasn't nearly as good at hiding it as you were," she added with a grin.

"I don't blame you for anything that happened seven years ago, not anymore. There's nothing more in the world I want than to be your wife and have another baby…or two, or three…with you. But I don't want you to quit working with Nick. I want to go back to Crystal Springs—with you, with my family. I want to go *home*, Connor."

"Are you sure?"

She didn't even have to think about it. With a nod, she said, "It might take some time. I might have to stay out here a while or fly back and forth until all the arrangements can be settled, but I think Danny will understand. He shouldn't have any problem finding a new partner to take my place in the firm."

Happiness blazed in his eyes, and she knew the same emotion had to be reflected on her own face.

"You know," he said in a low voice, shuffling forward so that she was forced to shuffle back, "we have a lot of lost time to make up for. Months. Years. A decade."

Her hip bumped the edge of her desk and she gave a startled yip when he lifted her onto the flat surface, moving between her legs. He nuzzled her neck, the sensitive spot behind her ear.

"As much as I'd like to, I do have a lunch appointment."

"Buzz your receptionist. Tell her to call and cancel."

His tongue darted out to lick a path of sensual fire from her collarbone to her cleavage and she moaned, letting her head fall back to grant him better access.

"I can't," she all but whimpered. "It's not even my client. I'm covering for Danny."

Bumping her knees farther apart, he pressed his arousal into the apex of her thighs. His busy fingers loosened the tail of her shirt from the waistband of her skirt.

"Then hold on to your law degree, sweetheart. You're about to be fashionably late."

So she did.

And she was.

* * * * *